Through Angel's Eyes

Through Angel's Eyes

by
Steve Theunissen

Strategic Book Publishing and Rights Co.

Strategic Book Publishing and Rights Co.
12620 FM 1960, Suite A4-507
Houston, TX 77065
www.sbpra.com

ISBN: 978-1-61897-374-0

Book Design by Julius Kiskis

20 19 18 17 16 15 14 13 12   1 2 3 4 5

Dedication

For Shelley, Chantel and Sasha—with love.

Acknowledgments

Martin Luther King, Junior: "Loving Your Enemies," Sermon at Dexter Avenue Baptist Church (11/17/1957), quoted on pp 128–130.

James Bevel: Address at Sixteenth Street Baptist Church (5/1/1963), quoted on pp 145–148.

Martin Luther King, Junior: "I Have A Dream," Speech at Washington, D.C. (8/28/1963), quoted on pp 280–283.

Prologue
ALABAMA 1960

I ain't never been able to figure some folks out. Like last summer, when me an' Rachel Colter went with her daddy for a trip into the big town. Why, me an' Rachel was so taken with all the sights an' noises an' colors an' all those folks. Rachel an' me said we'd be slave girls for a month a' Sundays jus' to have one a' those pretty dresses we seen on those White girls. But, I guess we shouldn'a been thinkin' like that, 'cause that's what led to the spoilin' part. An', anyway, when we told Rachel's daddy 'bout it on the way home, he said it was feelin's a' jealousy like what we had for them dresses that led some bad men to kill the Lord Jesus. I couldn't help thinkin' that if Jesus'd been a dirt-poor Black girl in Alabama, he'd sure like to have a fine white dress, jus' the same.

Anyways, after traipsin' 'round in the hot sun after Rachel's daddy while he was doin' his bidness, he took us to a candy store. Ya know, that store had candy everywhere. Why, that's all it had. Jus' candy. Not like the General Store in Harpersville, that only had two jars on the counter 'midst all the hardware an' stuff. Me and Rachel jus' wandered 'round lookin' at all the different kinds a' candy—orange ones, blue striped ones, even little animal shaped ones. Jus' as I was decidin' on what to buy with the nickel Rachel's daddy gave me, I seen this magnificent creature come into the store. Why, she was 'bout seventeen an' oh-so pretty. But the thing that got me was her dress. It actually sparkled. I ain't never seen nothin' like it to this day.

Anyways, next thing I knew I was goin' over to that White girl. I don't know what made me do it. It was sorta like a magnet pulled me over. She didn't notice me 'cause she was with some big handsome White boy who was whisperin' in her ear. So, I says to that White girl, "Scuse me ma'am, but that's a real pretty dress you got on."

Well, when that White girl turned an' looked down at me, I thought she'd jus' seen a rat crawlin' 'cross the floor. Her face curled up into a scowl an' she said to her boyfriend, all hysterical like, "Scott, what's that nigger doin' in here?"

So, straight away, Scott pulled her away from me, like I might give her some disease or somethin', an' he kneeled down in front a' me an' said, all angry like, "Nigger, git your Black behind outta here before we lose our appetite!"

Well, I seen lots a' things in big old Birmin'ham that day, but of all the sights an' sounds an' noises, there's only one word that's burnin' in my memory—NIGGER.

Chapter ONE
ALABAMA, JANUARY 1963

"What you readin' bout, Jimmy?"

"Just a story 'bout a man, Angel."

My brother Jimmy was always into readin' lately. Seems he was gettin' all these important ideas stirrin' 'round in his brain. When I told him that if he takes in much more, why, all those ideas was bound to spill outta his head, he jus' muttered somethin' 'bout readers bein' leaders an' knowledge is power.

"What sorta power you talkin' 'bout, Jimmy? Everyone here 'bouts knows that Daddy's the most powerful man in Harpersville an' he ain't never read a book in his life."

"Angel, you don't understan'. Daddy's a powerful strong man, that's for sure. But there ain't a Black man in this country who's got any real power, any influence in their community."

"What do ya want that sorta power for, Jimmy?"

"'Cause it's our due, Angel. We was born as free citizens a' this country and we have the right to all the benefits a' bein' a free citizen."

"I don't understan', Jimmy. Your books are makin' you sound like a school teacher or somethin'."

"Well it's like this, see. When you was born, it's like you was invited to a meal. There's this table spread out with all this beautiful food—chicken, turkey, roast taters, green beans an' the like. But when you turn up to take your place at the table, ya

1

find that your place has already been taken an' the folks kick you under the table an' tell ya to beg for your food."

"Why they do that?"

"Because we don't look like they do."

"You mean 'cause we're niggers, don't ya?"

Jimmy stopped readin' his book, placed it on the table an' looked at me for the first time since I walked into his room. I could tell he was thinkin' hard 'bout how to answer me.

"Angel," he began, "what you are is a beautiful, smart girl. Now there are a lot a' people out there who have a disease called prejudice, an' they want you to think that you're a no-account nigger who'll never amount to nothin'. But, girl, don't you ever believe that—not ever. You hear me?"

"Yes, Jimmy. But do ya reckon those folks will always have that disease?"

"Some folks will, Angel. But many of them have it 'cause it's always been there. It's part a' the system. Now, that system can be changed, but the change has to come from us."

"How though?"

"Well, that's what I'm readin' 'bout. The most powerful weapon is to have no weapon at all. Non-violent resistance could bring this country to its knees, just like it did in India."

There he went again, with all those funny ideas. I looked over at the book on Jimmy's bedside table: *A Life of M. K. Gandhi.*

"Jimmy," I said, "those books are makin' you crazy!"

†††

My daddy really was the most powerful man in Harpersville. He could whip any man in town an' I knew some folks who was right scared a' my pa. My brother Jimmy wasn't one of 'em. Daddy never did go in for learnin' an' such, an' it seemed like every idea that Jimmy was puttin' into his brain was 'specially designed to rile my pa. But whatever had gone before weren't nothin' compared to what happened the night Jimmy told the family he was helpin' some Black folks to get the vote. Daddy didn't take long to get riled.

"What'd ya jus' say, boy?" he demanded.

"Now, Daddy, jus' hear me out." Jimmy always tried that one first. He called it bein' diplomatic.

"No, son, you hear me out. Ya reckon ya know what it's all 'bout. You got some learnin', huh? Read some books, have ya?"

Daddy's temper was gettin' hotter with each word. I was gettin' scared, so I sank down in my chair an' looked down at the table, pretendin' that I wasn't there. But I couldn't escape Daddy's words.

"Well, let me tell ya some things ya ain't read about, boy. You ain't the first nigger to forget his place. Your gran'pappy, he thought he be a union man—takin' on the White bosses. Got hisself a bullet in the head, boy!" Daddy spat the words out, like they was burnin' in his mouth.

"And I'll tell ya somethin' else."

As he spoke, Daddy kicked away his chair an' stood over Jimmy. I thought Daddy was gonna hit him, an' I saw Jimmy flinch. But, instead, Daddy ripped off his own shirt. I let out a horrified moan as I stared at my beloved Daddy's upper body. Mama moved 'round the table an' cradled me in her arms.

"Have a look at your ol' man's back, boy," Daddy ordered.

Jimmy didn't say a word. At least he knew that. Anythin' he said now would be like pourin' fat on a fire. But Jimmy's eyes was busy. So was mine. Daddy had never took off his shirt in front of us before. Now we knew why. His back was a mess. It had four long black stripes 'cross it an' a whole lotta other scars criss-crossin' them. I had to look away.

"Take a good look, boy. This is what comes from your fancy ideas."

Daddy slumped back into his chair. His powerful chest was heavin' up an' down, but, strangely, his anger seemed to be coolin'. "Don't make me bury my son alongside my pa, boy." His words was softer, more controlled. "Don't try to be more than ya are—an Alabama nigger."

I got a shock when I saw my Daddy's back but what happened next was entirely unbelievable to me. As I was lookin' upon Daddy's face, his strong hard face, I saw a tear roll down his unshaven cheek. My Daddy was the most powerful man in Harpersville. He could whip any man in town. My Daddy didn't cry. But I saw it with my own eyes, an' before long, the tears was rollin' down my face, too.

†††

I was real confused. I didn't know why Daddy was so angry. I didn't know why Jimmy was gettin' so many uppity ideas. But, most of all, I didn't understan' why Daddy had called his own flesh an' blood a nigger. Why, Jimmy had said it was diseased White folks who called us niggers, not our own pa! So, I did what I always did when I got confused. I went down to ol' Miss Hattie's place so she could sort this mess out for me. Miss Hattie knew everythin' 'bout everyone that ever was an' she had a way 'bout her that jus' made ya understan' things. Why, I reckon she was as wise as ol' King Solomon hisself.

†††

Well, when I got into her yard, I seen her straight off. She was sittin' in her big ol' rockin' chair on the front porch. When I got closer, I called out, "Hi ya, Miss Hattie."

"Hi ya, yourself, little Angel Dunbar," she replied. "You decided to come brighten up an ol' lady's day?"

"Well, sorta," I said as I got up the steps onto the porch an' climbed onto her lap. I always felt so safe there—as if the big ol' world with its Birmin'ham towns, its nigger callin' diseased White folks an' its angry daddies all disappeared an' it was jus' me an' Miss Hattie an' her overgrown garden, forever.

"Something's troublin' ya, ain't it?" Miss Hattie could read me like a book.

"I've been all tied up like a bundle a' wool, Miss Hattie, jus' tryin' to figure out what's goin' on with Jimmy an' Daddy," I replied, glad to be lettin' it out. "They're so different. Why, ya know, Daddy called Jimmy a nigger last night."

I looked up into Miss Hattie's face then, expecting to see the look a' shock that I felt when I heard Daddy use that word. Instead, she smiled an' began strokin' my hair.

"Ya might think they're different girl," she said softly, "but your Daddy an' your brother are both the same. They're both like stallions. Your brother's like a wild stallion that won't let a bridle or a bit get near it, jus' like your pa was before he got broken in. Now he's a tamed stallion."

"I reckon Daddy was broke in with whips," I whispered.

"Why ya say that, girl?"

"'Cause I seen what they did to his back."

"You're right, girl. But, ya know, that father a' yours, he was fightin' the system jus' like your brother is. Only difference is, he fought it with his fists. Your brother is fightin' with his mind. Changin' it from within, ya know?"

"Sorta, Miss Hattie, but how's Jimmy gonna change things?"

"Well, Jimmy's workin' to give people the real power that counts—the power a' the vote."

"What's so important 'bout the vote?"

"Well girl, there's twenty million Black folks in the South. If we can vote, then we can get some folks in charge who'll start makin' things better for us."

"So, how we get the vote, Miss Hattie."

"Why, we gotta have the strength to jus' march on in there an' ask for it."

"That sounds easy."

"Ain't so, girl. White man got us folks so low down we can't even reach up to tie our boot straps."

"What ya mean, Miss Hattie?"

"Folks is scared, girl."

"Scared a' what?"

"Lots a' things—mostly change."

†††

What was I doin'? I must've been crazy! But, there I was, layin' on the back floor a' Jimmy's auto-car as it bumped an' rocked its way towards Birmin'ham town. How I wished I was back on Miss Hattie's porch, safely snuggled in her lap. But how could that be when Miss Hattie was sittin' in the front passenger seat all dressed up in her Sunday finery. My brother Jimmy was all dolled up too, with his white pressed shirt an' tie.

Why, when Jimmy told me he was takin' his first voter into the city to register, I got this fool idea to hide in the back a' his car, so I could see what all the fuss was 'bout. So there I was, hid under an ol' wool blanket. It was hotter than a bonfire under there, an' before long, I could taste the sweat on my lips. When Jimmy stopped to pick up his passenger, I waited to see if I could make out who it was from the voice. Well, when I heard that wise ol' owl's voice, it was all I could do to stop myself from screamin' out, "Miss Hattie!" But I still managed to stay hid, 'cause I wanted to see what was gonna happen more than ever now.

By an' by, we arrived into the city. I knew 'cause of all the noise from the cars an' people. But still, it seemed like we was drivin' for ages until the car finally came to a stop. After some talkin', I heard Jimmy an' Miss Hattie get out. I counted to fifty, goin' real slow, then ripped that blanket offa me. I got up on the back seat an' looked out the window. We was right in front of a real big white buildin' with a whole lotta steps out front. Above the doorway was a sign sayin' 'Jefferson County Court House'. I could jus' see Jimmy an' Miss Hattie goin' in through the doors.

In no time, I was outta that car an' racin' 'round the back a' that big ol' building. I got me up a pipe an' onto a window ledge. I looked inside an' saw a big brown desk in one corner a' the room. Behind it was a skinny lookin' ancient White man. He wore a grey suit an' had a serious look on his face. He was writin' in some important lookin' book. Next thin' I know, open goes the door an' in comes none other than my brother Jimmy an' Miss Hattie. The man looked up angrily.

"What ya want, boy!" he barked at Jimmy.

"I've brought this lady down to register," Jimmy said, all respectful like. The man turned his head in Miss Hattie's direction. An ugly grin came 'cross his face that reminded me a' that White girl in the candy store when she'd looked down at me.

"What ya want to register for, old woman?" he snapped.

Miss Hattie looked him right in the eyes an' said, "Because I am just as much a citizen a' this country as you are."

"You read?" he shot back.

"As long as it's in English," Miss Hattie answered, smilin'.

The man reached into his desk drawer an' pulled out a big sheet a paper, which he threw on the desk in front a' him.

"Go out in the hall and fill this out then," he demanded.

Miss Hattie took the form an' slowly left the room. When she'd closed the door behind her, the White man fixed a mean stare on Jimmy. I could feel his anger an' I felt scared for my brother. I wanted to jump through that window an' tell that skinny ol' White man to have some manners an' treat folks nicer. Instead, I pressed my nose up harder to the window an' kept listenin'.

"Who are you to bring people down here to register, boy?"

"It's my job."

"Suppose you get two bullets in the head right now!"

"I got to die anyhow."

"Suppose someone came in that door right now and shot you in the head—right now—what would you do?"

"I couldn't do nothin'. But the whole world'd be on your doorstep tomorrow."

"Who'll tell 'em?"

"The people I work for."

"Listen, boy," the man was actually yellin' now. "I've had enough of your uppity nigger ideas. Git your Black hide outta my office an' get back to your shanty town—where you belong!"

Jus' then, Miss Hattie came back in an' placed the form on the mans' desk.

"See you on votin' day," she said as her an' Jimmy left the room.

†††

I was back under that ol' wool blanket. We was bumpin' an' rockin' our way back to Harpersville, where we belonged. As Jimmy an' Miss Hattie spoke 'bout things like this bein' a land-mark day an' how we'll see a rush to the vote now that Miss Hattie has shown the way, all I could think 'bout was how hot it was under that blanket. Why, it was so hot I thought I was gonna die under there. After a while I could feel the heat chokin' me up inside, makin' it hard to even breathe. I so much wanted to kick off that blanket!

I guess that's what us Black folks is under—a big ol' blanket that's pressin' down on us, nearly suffocatin' us. Most Black folks don't even try to get it off. Some folks, like my pa, try to rip it away, but they get beat down. Others, like Jimmy, try to sorta unstitch it, but White folks try to stop them, too. I wish White folks would understan'. We don't wanna throw the blanket over you. We jus' wanna get it off us, so we can breathe. That ain't askin' too much, is it?

Well, I reckon that White girl in the candy store an' that court man sure reckon it is. I suppose I'll never be able to figure some folks out.

Chapter TWO
ALABAMA, FEBRUARY 1963

I was scribblin' again. I jus' couldn't help it. Mister Newton's voice was so soft an' gentle, an' the story so borin', that my mind sorta skipped over to thinkin' a' cartoons an' my hand jus' naturally followed. Next thing, I was drawin' a big ol' circle on my page, with black, fuzzy curls on top. Every time I drew a cartoon a' Mister Newton, it'd end up lookin' like one a' those fancy pug dogs I seen a rich lady leadin' 'round the streets a' Birmin'ham once. I used to think how nice it'd be to swap places with one a' those dogs, jus' for a day. I thought 'bout all the cooin' an' cuddlin' those White folks give to dumb animals, an' how it was so desperately needed by real life human bein's.

Human bein's like the ones sittin' 'round me at the Harpersville Schoolhouse. There was Josiah Reeby, hunched over his desk. I never knew why he looked so sad, so far away, until my brother told me Josiah's story—a story 'bout a drunken father, a strugglin' mother, a terrible fight an' a ambulance that never arrived. It left Josiah with no mother, a broken father an' three younger brothers who needed somethin' more. Josiah was doin' his best, tryin' to keep things together an' stay normal. But his eyes was his give-away—they was dead. Thirteen years old an' dead eyes. He sure could take the place a' one a' those rich White folk's dogs.

There was thirty-five Josiahs in that room. We all had different stories an' we all had our own sorry background. Then there was Mister Newton, with his chubby face an' his easy smile. He was always up there, at the front a' the class, his arms wavin' 'round, tryin' to get his bunch a' misfits excited 'bout algebra or spellin' or somethin'. I knew Mister Newton was a good man. He talked to us like we was jus' the same as him, not like some a' the teachers who'd treat ya like trash. An' we weren't scared a' Mister Newton. I guess we could talk easy with him, like he was a big brother. But all a' us kids had a respect for him, jus' the same.

Mister Newton was sittin' at the front a' the room, readin' out chapter four a' *Tom Brown's Schooldays*. I concentrated on my cartoon, fillin' in the bulgy eyes, the droopy cheeks, then workin' down to the generous tummy an' podgy legs. I was jus' startin' to work on Mister Newton's stubby toes when a voice from behind me broke the steady sound a' Mister Newton's voice. All our heads twisted 'round to see who it was that'd interrupted our drowsy thoughts. Our eyes fixed on Ronny Jackson.

He was the new kid in our class. He'd moved into the little house on the corner a' Fifth Avenue an' Main with his mama an' two little sisters only two weeks back. Whenever we'd had new kids in our class before they was real quiet an' shy an' kept to themselves. Well, whatever Ronny Jackson was, it sure wasn't quiet an' shy. Why, jus' the second day he was with us, he cussed at Mister Newton. From then on it seemed like he'd gotten sure a' hisself an' he jus' 'bout did or said somethin' every day to cause a stir or upset things. Now I ain't never seen Mister Newton get real angry with any kids, an' he don't even have a switch in the classroom. So, when it came to dealin' with Ronny, Mister Newton was his ol' calm, patient self. After the first week a' havin' Ronny with us, I began thinkin' that maybe a switch in the class wouldn't be such a bad idea after all.

"Why we gotta listen to all that stuff 'bout English schoolin' for?" Ronny blurted out. "We ain't in Englan', we's in 'Merica!"

My eyes shot from Ronny 'cross the room to Mister Newton. *Finally, Ronny Jackson*, I almos' said out loud, *after two weeks you finally come out with somethin' sensible.* For Ronny jus' asked a question that I been too scared to ask for the las' month, ever since Mister Newton'd told us we'd be studyin' the English classics. Mister Newton stopped his readin' an' looked up, fixing his eyes on Ronny.

"Ronny," he began, his voice soundin' jus' a little annoyed, "I don't appreciate being rudely interrupted when I'm reading, and I'm sure no one else in this room does either. But, seeing as how you've asked a half way intelligent question for the first time since you've been in my classroom, I'll ignore you're rudeness this time."

That was Mister Newton all over. Most other teachers would've sprung outta their chairs, marched down to that Ronny Jackson, an' given him a thick ear for interruptin' their readin'. I always thought Mister Newton handled things like a real gentleman, an' I respected him even more for it. He continued, this time his voice remindin' me a' how my brother Jimmy talked to me when he was tryin' to explain somethin' real important.

"Now, I know you kids don't have much in common with Tom Brown, but, son, that's the whole point. The beauty of books is that you can travel to other places, learn about different cultures, different ways of doing things, different types of people and their experiences. And what you learn is bound to help you in your own life. Don't you agree, Ronny?"

All eyes now moved back to Ronny. His eyes was fixed on the teacher, like he'd been listenin' real hard to Mister Newton's answer, an', for the first time, I realized that this boy wasn't silly. What he said next proved it.

"Sure, we can learn from books," he said, "but why not ones 'bout us, like *Uncle Tom's Cabin* or somethin'? That'll help us more than learnin' 'bout some place we ain't never gonna get to."

Lookin' back at Mister Newton, I could tell he was surprised at how sensible Ronny's answer was, too. He stood up, moved over to his desk, an' put *Tom Brown's Schooldays* down. He leaned on the edge a' his desk an' folded his arms across his chest as he stretched out his legs in front a' him, the way I seen him do hundreds a' times before.

"When you kids see me up here," he began, speakin' so kindly an' caringly, not jus' to Ronny now, but to the whole class, "I guess you see me as representing the whole education system. And so you should, because I'm probably the only part of it you'll ever come into contact with. But, in reality, I'm only one small part of that system. At the top of the education system is the Board of Education, and it's that Board that sorts out the curriculum of all schools, including this one. It tells us what we need to cover in algebra, the history subjects to be taught and even the books to be read. Now, Ronny Jackson, here, believes that *Uncle Tom's Cabin* would be a far greater learning experience for this class than *Tom Brown's Schooldays*. Well, let me tell you something, Ronny, I agree with you, and, if it was up to me, that's exactly what we'd be reading. But, you see, my job is to teach the curriculum as set by the Board of Education. So, if they say *Tom Brown's Schooldays* and if you want to pass your end of year finals, then *Tom Brown's Schooldays* it is."

"Sounds like those folks up there at the Board a' Education don't care so much 'bout teachin' Black folks what's important." Ronny spat the words out. "How many Black folks on that there Board anyway, Mister Newton?"

"There are none, Ronny," Mister Newton said with a little smile. Then, speakin' to the whole class again, "It seems that

Ronny has brought up an area that's been waiting quietly to be addressed for some time now—something that's actually very dear to my heart. The school curriculum contains many important things—things that you all need in order to become adults that can contribute to our society. Of course, you also need these things to be able to pass your end of year examinations."

Mister Newton moved away from his desk now, an' began pacin' 'cross the front a' the room.

"But there are other things," he continued, "things unique to us as Afro-Americans that are just as important, maybe, in a way, even more so, that are not part of this curriculum and that you children deserve to have. Problem is, how can you get both in just six hours a day?"

I had a feelin' from his voice that Mister Newton already had the answer, but it was his way to let us think we could come up with it ourselves.

"We could come to school earlier," called out Bernice Palmer from two rows in front a' me.

It was jus' like her to be saying somethin' like that, her bein' a brain-box an' all. Half a dozen voices soon made it clear what a bad idea that was. Sure, we wouldn't mind learnin' some stuff 'bout Black folks, but not if it meant getting outta bed any earlier.

"How 'bout stayin' later," suggested Amie Reynolds, from behind me.

I immediately thought a' Josiah Reeby an' knew that wasn't a good idea, neither. At three o'clock, Josiah had to put away childish things an' step back into the real world. It wouldn't wait for no extra schoolin'. Then Ronny's voice sounded out from behind me again.

"Best thing for everyone'd be to cut into our break times," he said, as if the other suggestions had been stupid. "That way nobody misses out on account a' what they gotta do at home."

An' that's how it happened. Mister Newton gave us all a note to take home to our folks tellin' all 'bout our Afro-American studies an' asking permission for us to take part. He made it real clear that 'cause this wasn't part a' the curriculum, we didn't have to do it if we'd rather play in the schoolyard at break time. But, the next Monday at ten thirty the yard was empty an' we all began learnin' 'bout ourselves. An' it was all thanks to that loudmouth in the corner, Ronny Jackson.

†††

The rush to vote that Jimmy said was gonna follow Miss Hattie's trip to the court was more like a trickle than a rush. Jimmy an' his friend Peter Lewis tried to get folks motivated, but, like Jimmy said, the hardest thing to overcome is fear a' man, an' fear a man—actually fear a' White man—was what the folks in Mason County ate, slept an' breathed. Jimmy an' Peter went 'round knocking on doors, puttin' notices on car windows an' even talkin' to church groups. Most folks wouldn't listen. Some slammed doors in their faces. Others agreed with what they said, but didn't wanna get involved. Jimmy told me that when he told ol' Mister Hanson on Seventh Street that he'd been involved ever since he'd been born as a Black man, why ol' Mister Hanson pointed his walkin' cane at Jimmy, shook it an' said, "Boy, da' Klan's got ways a' fixin' fas' mouthed nigras'. Quit it, afore yuh git yuhself kilt."

But Jimmy was never one for taking other folk's advice, 'specially when he knew he was right. So him an' Peter went right on trudgin' down dusty roads, knockin' on creaky cabin doors an' gettin' a whole lotta nothin' from the folks they was tryin' to help. It made me feel proud a' my brother that he'd keep on goin', keep on tryin' to make a difference. But it also made me feel sorry for him. I wanted to help him, to go with him up to those doors an' say to those scared folks, "You jus' gotta get the vote, Mister so an' so, 'cause that's the only way we gonna be free."

So I made a plan. I was gonna get out there with Jimmy an' show those folks that there ain't nothin' to be scared of. But there was jus' one thing that stood between my plan an' them folks gettin' registered—my brother Jimmy. He wouldn't have a lick of it. But, I guess, I was too much like him. I ain't been one to listen to other folks advice, too—'specially when I know I'm right. So I told him he was soundin' jus' like ol' Mister Hanson with his walkin' cane. But that brother a' mine sure was a stubborn ol' thing. He said I ain't comin' an' that's final. But that didn't make me give up. I kept on naggin' Jimmy 'bout it for a whole two weeks until, finally, he said I could come with him that Sataday mornin', but I was most definitely not allowed to say nothin'. Not one word. Jus' stand there, be polite an' observe.

So, there I was again—in the back a' Jimmy's car headin' off into the unknown. Actually, we was headin' out to the sharecroppin' village 'bout two miles outta town. All the way there, my heart was poundin' inside a' me. I tried to tell myself not to be stupid an' calm down. But, I jus' couldn't stop that heart from poundin'. As we pulled up at the beginnin' a' the village, I said to my brother, "Jimmy, I ain't feelin' good 'bout this."

"Don't worry, Angel, everything's gonna be fine. We're jus' gonna go over there an' have a nice chat with those folks, then we'll move on, okay?"

Jimmy's voice was so soft an' comfortin' that it jus' 'bout calmed me down. 'Least it was enough to get me climbin' outta that car an' followin' him to the first house, anyways. I looked 'round the dusty road. The kids that'd been playing with an ol' tire had left it lyin' on the road an' taken off when they saw us gettin' outta the car. They left the whole place seemin' too quiet.

The houses 'round there didn't have no fences. You couldn't hardly tell where the dirt an' clay road ended an' the folk's yards started. Anyways, the front yards was jus' patches a' sunbaked dirt, with a few hunks a' dead grass spread 'bout. I thought that those kids must have real hard heads an' bodies to be jumpin' 'round an' skippin', like kids do, on that hard ground. I looked up at the house in front a' me. No paint on the wallboards. Newspaper coverin' one window. Bottom window on the door smashed. Three broken boards on the steps. I put all these things together in my mind an' realized that I already knew some things 'bout the people livin' in that house—poor folks, hard workin', but never really makin' it.

Jimmy jumped over the broken steps an' onto the porch. He knocked three times loudly on the top glass window a' the front door. Straight away, I heard a baby start cryin'. *"Good start Jimmy,"* I thought. I bit my lip, waiting for some fat ol' woman to rip open that door an' start yellin' at Jimmy 'bout how she's been tryin' to get that kid to sleep for the last hour. But no one came, so Jimmy knocked again. Now, the cryin' a' the baby was gettin' louder. I heard an inside door open, an' then the noise a' someone comin' closer. The door opened an' a man 'bout the same age as Daddy stood in front of us.

He was a hard lookin' man with big hands an' a face that jus' told you he'd seen plenty a' sufferin'. He was wearing a pair a' dungarees an' suspenders. His arms an' shoulders was bare, 'cept for his suspender straps. I admired the muscles a' his arms, thinkin' 'bout the long hours in the field tendin' crops an' how they'd shaped him into a powerful piece a' man.

"Hello sir, my name's James Dunbar," my brother said as he reached out his hand to shake.

"Whatcha want?" the man shot back, without even offerin' his hand.

"Well," Jimmy began, "we've been talkin' to folks about some a' the laws that make it hard for us folks—"

"'I ain't lookin' to get involved in none a' that law stuff," the man cut him off. "We got enough problems right here, right now."

"We aren't here to bring any trouble, Mister," Jimmy said in his politest voice. "We're here to help folks to help themselves. Can I explain how?"

"Boy, you know what?" The man was getting angry now. "If Mister Charley comes a drivin' down that road an' sees me talkin' to you, what you think he's gonna do? He's gonna pull this here job, this house an' this stinkin' life right from under me. Now, it reckons to me, best way I can help myself is to quit talkin' fool ideas with the likes a' you!"

He reached across to the door handle an' began to pull it towards him. As the door was closin', Jimmy pulled a sheet a' paper from his pocket an' passed it to the man.

"There's a meetin' tomorrow at seven p.m. to discuss voter registration. Please—"

That's as far as Jimmy got before the door slammed. An' that was the story of our mornin'. Some houses, folks wouldn't even answer the doors. We knew they was home on account a' the kids yellin'. Those that did come to the door acted like we was they enemy, instead a' they friends tryin' to help 'em out. They was jus' plain scared. Scared to get involved. It reminded me 'bout what Miss Hattie'd said to me that time—folks are mostly scared a' change. But lookin' 'round at the kinda life these folks had, I would have thought they'd welcome a change.

As we drove home, without gettin' so much as one person who was willin' to even listen to Jimmy's talk 'bout registerin', I began to realize that folks could only be helped if they want to. If they don't really wanna be free, there ain't nothing me or Jimmy or any other person can do 'bout it. An' goin' by what I seen that day, I reckoned that most Black folks was right happy to jus' carry on with things like they'd always been. It sorta reminded me of a blind man who'd never been able to see, so didn't even miss it an' was jus' happy to go on bein' blind. It was only later that I realized that every single one a' those folks that'd pushed us away that day really did have a rage for freedom in their belly. It was jus' gonna take a little more time to let it out.

†††

"Who has heard of George Washington?" was how Mister Newton began our Afro-American class that Monday.

'Bout twenty hands shot up.

"Very good, people," he said. "Now who has heard of Crispus Attucks?"

There was a puzzled silence an' not one hand went up.

"Who's heard of Abraham Lincoln?"

Most a' the class put their hand up.

"What about Harriet Tubman?"

This time all the hands stayed down.

Mister Newton was gettin' at somethin' here. We'd all read stories 'bout Washin'ton an' Lincoln in our textbooks. But who was these other folks he was askin' 'bout? An' why should we have heard of 'em? Mister Newton explained.

"George Washington was the man who led America into independence. But the first man to give his life over to that cause, the first martyr for the freedom of this nation, was a man who has been left out of the history books."

He turned to the blackboard an' wrote Crispus Attucks on it. He then turned back to us.

"Abraham Lincoln was the Sixteenth President of the United States. He steered the nation through its darkest years—years of terrible civil war. And it was his signature that put an end to slavery. But years before Lincoln gave us our freedom, a heroic woman was helping hundreds of folks to claim it for themselves. Her name has been lost to history. It deserves to be known."

Again, he turned to the board. This time he wrote Harriet Tubman.

"Now, why were these people left out of the history books," he asked. "Who thinks they know?"

I looked 'round at the other kids. Most of 'em looked confused, jus' like I was. How we meant to know why those folks from hundreds a' years ago with the funny names weren't in the history books? An' what's that got to do with our studies 'bout Black folks?

When he saw that no one was gonna put up their hand, Mister Newton reached over to his desk an' picked up two drawings a' people's faces. He also grabbed the sticky tape. He stuck the drawings alongside the names he'd jus' written on the board. I studied the pictures. The man looked in his middle thirties. He had a hard look to his face. The woman looked tough, too. She had the face of a worker an' her head was covered in a scarf. Apart from that, they looked as different as any two people I could think of. Except, a'course, for one other thing—one thing that made everythin' Mister Newton was sayin' make sense. They were both Black.

"Both of these people made historic contributions to the United States of America," Mister Newton said, "but their contributions have been lost to history for one simple reason—because they were Afro-Americans. Today we're going to put the value of their lives on the map—at least the map of this classroom."

"Mister Newton, why they been left out?"

It was Bernice Palmer who asked the question. It didn't surprise me. She had her nose stuck in books so much she mustn't a' noticed that Black folks didn't count in this country—never had. I pricked up my ears, waitin' to see how Mister Newton would handle this one.

"Well, Bernice," he said, "up until 1863 Afro-Americans were brought to America, not as human beings, but as property, as slaves. So, in the reckoning of history, they didn't exist as people. So they couldn't have a part in the shaping of our history. It's as simple as that."

"What happened in 1863?" asked Jimmy Thorpe.

"That was the year that the President, Mister Lincoln, signed of piece of paper called the Emancipation Proclamation. It put an end to slavery and put the negroes of America on the road to freedom."

Then I recognized Ronny Jackson's voice from behind me. His words had a sorta mockin' sound to them.

"How far we come down that road, Mister Newton?"

Mister Newton looked across at Ronny, with jus' the hint of a smile on his face.

"Well Ronny," he said, "if you'd been a slave in the 1860s, I'm sure you'd agree that we've come quite a way."

"That right?" Ronny spat out.

The way he said those two words caused every head in that room to turn an' look at him. I noticed Ronny rock back in his chair an' I could tell he was enjoyin' the full attention a' the class. He waited for a moment, then asked, "What say the great grandson a' that Attucks fella walked into the lunch counter at Woolworths an' asked for a coffee? What do ya reckon'd happen to him, Mister Newton?"

"He'd be removed son," Mister Newton replied, sitting on the corner a' his desk.

"Yeah, well what 'bout if he said to those White fellas, 'Jus' a minute, Mister White Man, there's somethin' ya don't understan'. My great grandpappy was the first man to get hisself killed so you all can be free. So don't you think you better get me my coffee?' What'd happen to him then, Mister Newton?"

"Ronny, you've made a very eloquent point," Mister Newton said, his voice more powerful than before. "Now we all know that the freedom promised in the Emancipation Proclamation has been slow in coming—in many ways it still hasn't come. I'm not going to stand up here and deny that. But let's start doing something about that situation by helping ourselves. And today we're helping ourselves by learning about our heritage. Is that all right with you, Mister Jackson?"

"You really want us to help ourselves?" Ronny shot back.

"That's what I said, son."

"Then lets learn from that Attucks fella an' go out there an' take our freedom jus' like him an' those others did at the Revolution."

"Ronny!" Mister Newton was gettin' tired a' this now. "You cannot compare the overthrow of the yoke of colonialism with the struggle for racial equality. They are completely separate issues."

"Easy for you to say. But how 'bout this?" Ronny was goin' for it now, like he was jus' gettin' warmed up before. He was gonna have his say an' no one was gonna stop him.

"Washin'ton an' them was like slaves to the English. But they had enough guts to pick up a gun an' kick those English fellas out. If they didn't do that, we'd still be slaves to Englan'. So if Black folks wanna be free there's only one way it's gonna happen—by picking up a gun jus' like ol' George Washin'ton an' that Attucks fella did."

"Ronny you listen to me," Mister Newton said with a sharpness to his voice that took me by surprise. "To fight for the independence of a country is one thing. But to fight so you can live in peace with those that you're fighting against? Think about it, son, it doesn't make any sense. And besides, negroes in this country are outnumbered ten to one. We'd be committing racial suicide to go down the road of violence in order to get equality."

"Sounds like you jus' another scared nigger to me."

Ronny said those words half under his breath, but they was loud enough to sound out right 'round that room. When I heard the words I made a wincin' kinda sound like I jus' been kicked in the belly. *Ronny Jackson*, I thought, *you jus' don't know when enough's enough, do ya? Mister Newton was only trying to make ya understan' somethin'. No need to go off an' call him somethin' like that.*

"All right, boy, you've had your say." Mister Newton's voice interrupted my thoughts. It was the angriest I ever heard him. "Now these other children gave up their playing time to learn something this morning. And as it seems none of us will be allowed to learn anything in your presence, I'll ask you to leave this room right now and stay away from our Afro-American classes until you can have some positive input. You can return to normal classes when you hear the bell ring."

Ronny didn't move an inch. Jus' sat there starin' at Mister Newton—darin' him to make the next move.

"Now," was all that Mister Newton said.

He didn't say it angry or loud or hysterical. It was actually so soft that I could hardly hear it. But when I looked back at Ronny, he was already gettin' outta his chair. I wondered if he'd slam the door on his way out. He didn't disappoint me. We never saw him for a whole three days after that.

✝✝✝

"When's this thing gonna start, Jimmy?" I asked my brother for the third time.

I was sittin' on the floor a' the youth club in Birmin'ham. It was pretty uncomfortable down there, squashed up amongst 'bout thirty other kids, mostly older than me. I tried crossin' my legs at first, but after 'bout ten minutes I started to gettin' the cramp, so now I was kneelin'. Before long, I felt my foot goin' to sleep again. I started to thinkin' that maybe I shouldn't've bothered Jimmy so much 'bout what he was gettin' into. Lord knows, I could sure do without having doors slammed in my face, an' now bein' made to sit 'round on a cold floor all night waitin' for who knows what to happen. I glanced up at the clock on the wall. Ten to nine. Why, I could be stretched out on my bed right 'bout now, readin' a comic book or somethin'.

"Soon enough," was all that Jimmy said.

For the tenth time my eyes moved across the banner that'd been hung on the wall, jus' below the scoreboard.

STUDENT NON-VIOLENT COORDINATING COMMITTEE

I wondered what those words meant. I knew what a student was—a kid who went to school. An' the word non-violent reminded me a' the argument between Mister Newton an' Ronny on Monday. I remembered Mister Newton sayin' how it'd be like committin' suicide to follow the way a' violence. So, he must believe in non-violence. Well, I wondered if Mister Newton knew 'bout the Student Non-Violent Coordinatin' Committee. Sounds maybe somethin' he'd like. So, I made up my mind to tell him all 'bout it on Monday.

Next thing I knew, two men came outta the men's changin' room. They walked to the middle a' the court, right in front a' all a' us, an' one of 'em sat on a chair that'd been put up there for him.

The other fella stood in front of us an' rubbed his hands together.

"Friends, let me apologize for the delay tonight," he began. "We've been driving down from Ohio and we had a few unscheduled delays. So, I'd like to thank you all for your patience and now let's get underway."

He had a nice soundin' voice, this fella. It was warm an' invitin', like Mister Newton's. But it was also confident, like he was real sure a' hisself. He had the look a' confidence 'bout him, too. He must've been in his early twenties, not that much older than Jimmy. He had a sharp lookin' face with high cheekbones. His face hadn't seen a razor for a couple a' days an' he looked real tired. He wore a white t-shirt with the letters SNCC written 'cross his chest. Faded jeans an' old sneakers completed his outfit.

"My name's Dave Richmond and I'd like to welcome you all and thank you for coming tonight," he said as he looked 'round the room. "Now, let me tell you all a little story. Not long ago, I was with some other boys in Greensboro, North Carolina. We decided one day that we were hungry so we went and sat down at the Woolworth's lunch counter. Now, we weren't meant to be at that counter on account of us bein' Black. See, we weren't human enough to sit in the same room as White folks. Why, we mighta spoilt their meals."

Those words caught my attention. My mind raced back to that candy store an' the hate-filled words a' that White boy, Scott, tellin' me that I was spoilin' his appetite. An' now, here was this fella from a thousan' miles away saying the same sorta thing'd happened to him. From that moment on, I forgot 'bout the cramp in my foot an' concentrated on every word comin' outta this fella's mouth.

"Well, to tell you all the truth we didn't know what to expect and we were all mighty scared," he said. "There was this policeman standing behind us, pounding his club into his palm, lookin' as menacing as possible. We looked over to the store manager, jus' waiting for him to come over and throw us out. We waited for one of them—the policeman or the manager—to put an end to our little show. Slowly it began to dawn on us."

He paused for a moment, jus' long enough for us to wonder what it was that'd dawned on them.

"Because we hadn't provoked the policeman,' he explained, 'he didn't know what to do with us. And because we weren't a threat and to avoid creating a public disturbance, the manager thought it best to jus' ignore us. On that day, friends, the First of February, 1960, four nigger boys brought a three hundred year old system of segregation to a standstill."

All the other kids in the room began clappin' then, so I joined in. It was a loud, short clap, an' it got a thankful smile from the speaker.

"Well, we sat there for over an hour that day,' he continued , 'and we got plenty of abuse from White folks passing by. But, after a while, I saw this elderly White lady making her way straight over towards me. She had white gloves on. Well, when she got close, she put her hand on mine, squeezed it tight and said, 'Boys, you should have done this ten years ago!' I can still remember the feel of those silky gloves and the power of those few words."

His voice was sorta faraway now, an' I could tell that he'd really been touched by that ol' White lady. Then he switched back to us.

"Well, friends, in the years since then, what we did has come to be known as sit-ins and about fifty thousand people, both Black and White, have been a part of them. The result? Segregation is on the way out! Hundreds of lunch counters, from as far apart as Texas and Georgia, have been desegregated."

He then went on to tell us 'bout how the Student Non-Violent Coordinatin' Committee had come 'bout. How young leaders stood up outta the sit-in movement an' came together to form what he called a direct action non-violent coordinatin' group to bring all the student groups in the different states together, so they'd be stronger. His talk was gettin' kinda technical for me an' I was startin' to get lost with all a' his big words. So, I was kinda glad when he introduced the other fella, who was sitting behind him. I hoped he weren't no big worder, like his friend. This fella was shorter an' rounder than the other one. He seemed like a happy an' bubbly type. I liked him right off.

"The sit-ins started at Woolworth's in Greensboro, jus' like Dave said," he began, in a cheery, high pitched voice, "but if it weren't for two things, they never would have been the kind of success we're seeing now. Who picked up what they were when Dave was talking to ya?"

This fella was good. He must've seen some of us losing attention at the end a' Dave's talk. So now he was gettin' us involved, askin' questions. I looked 'round an' saw four hands go up, all older kids. Jimmy's was the first.

"Sorry, I don't know your names. Can you jus' give that to us before you answer?" the guy at the front said.

He pointed to Jimmy first, so my brother said, "Jim's my name. Well, Dave said that because they weren't doing anything harmful, the policeman didn't know what to do with them."

"That's right, Jim," the man replied. "Not doing anything harmful, not being violent, not being pro-voc-a-tive." He stretched the word out, like he was havin' fun with it. "Not inciting any retaliation. That was a key to the success of the first sit-in. The key of non-violent resistance. What's the other key that led to the success of that first sit-in? Now, this one's a little trickier."

It took 'bout half a minute before anyone made a try at this one. Finally, a skinny fella who must've been 'bout seventeen put up his hand. The fella at the front nodded his head towards him.

"What do you think, friend?" he asked.

"Well, my name's Rosco, and I was jus' gonna say that it took the guts of them fellas to stop talking 'bout what was wrong and stand up and do somethin' 'bout it.

"You got it, Rosco," the fella at the front replied, "and that's what you call direct action. Some folks call it militancy. Getting up and confronting the system, but doing it in a passive, non-violent way. You know, that is the way to bring this Jim Crow system to its knees. But, why do you think non-violence is such an important tool?"

As he asked that question, he stretched his arms out, like he was invitin' us all to have a share in answerin'. The hands went up an' the answers came quick.

"Tom. Because it's non-provocative. It doesn't give them a reason to be violent to you."

"Joanne. Because it goes straight to the conscience of the enforcer."

"Arnold. Because it reflects the moral purity a' the cause."

"Johnny. Because it demonstrates to the whole world how unfair the system is that we've been suffering under for centuries."

"Very good, folks," said the speaker. "So, non-violent resistance is the cornerstone of our movement. And when you couple quiet, respectful non-violent resistance with determined militancy, you have a real force for change. But, I'm not going to kid you all. This sort of stuff ain't easy. It requires an amazing degree of determination and self-discipline. That's why we have what we call a self-purification program before we stage any demonstration. The self-purification program is basically a workshop where we can train ourselves, testing ourselves out in the way of non-violent direct action."

This fella talked on for the best part a' thirty minutes. He spoke 'bout the things that'd been learned from the demonstrations across the country. 'Bout how violent the police could get, how hate-filled the White crowds could be an' how condemnin' the local papers usually were. But he also spoke 'bout good things, like how the national papers was usually on our side, 'bout how many White folks'd been won over by the courage a' the demonstrators. An' he spoke 'bout a man who'd come out of a bus boycott in Montgomery, a man who was at the front a' the movement, leadin' it on, showin' the way. He was a man whose name I never heard before that day. A man whose name was to become as familiar as my own. A man called Martin Lutha' King, Junior.

Chapter THREE
ALABAMA, MARCH 1963

"You ever heard a' Martin Lutha' King?" I asked Miss Hattie dreamily.

It was a Sunday afternoon an' I was propped up on the railin' a' Miss Hattie's porch balcony. The sun was beatin' down real hard out in the yard. I felt lucky to have the shade a' that porch to cover me.

Ever since that Friday night my mind'd been filled with what those two fellas had talked 'bout. My thoughts led to questions an' my questions led to Miss Hattie. I knew she'd have the answers I needed.

"Where'd you learn 'bout Doctor King?" Miss Hattie replied quickly, like she was surprised at my question. She was sittin' in her rockin' chair, rockin' back an' forth like she didn't have a care in the world.

"What you mean, Miss Hattie?" She was gettin' me confused. "This fella I mean ain't no doctor or nothin'. He's a SNICK man."

"A what?"

"You know, a SNICK man."

This was the first time I had to explain somethin' to Miss Hattie.

"The Student Nonviolence Committee."

After a while, the two fellas at the meetin'd got tired a' usin' the full name so they jus' called themselves SNICK. It was easier for me to remember, too. Miss Hattie smiled in an understandin' kinda way.

"Oh, we're talking 'bout the same fella all right. The Reverend Doctor Martin Luther King, Junior. But he ain't no doctor a' medicine an' he ain't no SNICK man, neither."

Miss Hattie went on to tell me that there are people who can become doctors of other things than healin' folks. Doctor King was a doctor a' religion. Even though she explained it real good, it still seemed strange to me. A doctor who wasn't no doctor at all. I was still muddlin' over that one when she went on to explain that Doctor King wasn't a part a' SNICK, but he was the leader of another outfit called the Southern Christian Leadership somethin' or other. His org'nization was bigger an' had more church folks in it. They was supportin' an' helpin' the SNICK folks who was all much younger.

"Why they have all those organizations with all those big names for, anyway, Miss Hattie?" I asked.

"Well girl, you know when you get a cut on your skin when you're peelin' taters?"

"Yeah," I replied, wonderin' what that had to do with anythin'.

"Well, you might forget 'bout that cut an' maybe it won't bother you for a while. But, when you go out an' play an' you get dirt in that cut, what happens?"

"Well, it sorta starts to hurt an' goes all red, but what's that got to—?"

"An' then it gets this yellow stuff in it called puss, don't it?" she cut me off. " An' if you don't get it seen to, that there sore is gonna keep right on irritating you until it bursts an' all that puss an' blood an' dirt comes gushing out."

I winced at the thought.

"Now, it may not burst right away, but it's sure to do it someday, girl."

"Miss Hattie!" I had no idea what she was talkin' 'bout.

"Listen, girl, that cut is like what happened to Black folks hundreds a' years ago. They was living their own lives way off in Africa, not bothering anybody. Then the slave ships came an' carried them over here to America, where they've been slaves ever since. Over the centuries little bits a' dirt got into the cut, irritating it. First, it was White folks called abolitionists, then some Black people who wanted to change things their own way. Folks like Nat Turner an' Harriet Tubman."

"I know her, Miss Hattie," I cut in. "Mister Newton learned us 'bout her. She started up an underground railway for slaves."

"She sure did, Angel. An' she's a woman we can be proud of. It was folks like her that led to the first bursting a' that sore. You know when that was?"

"Suppose at the Southern War."

"That's right. An' that bursting let out a lot a' the diseased stuff under the skin. But it didn't heal the cut. Now, a hundred years later, more dirt has got in to irritate it, it's gone all red again an' a whole lot a' puss has built up. It's all set to burst again, girl."

"An' the bits a' dirt are those org'nizations like Southern Christian an' SNICK," I said, feelin' proud to have figured out what cuts an' sores had to do with the question I asked.

"Not quite, Angel. Those organizations are like the puss that comes as a result a' the dirt. You know, if you treat that cut a' yours better in the first place an' looked after it, you wouldn't get any dirt in it an' none a' the other things would happen, right?"

"Yeah."

"Well, White folks have been treating us so bad, its sorta like goin' out in the yard an' rolling in mud. A'course you'll get dirt in the wound. See, the dirt in the wound is the things that irritate this system that White folks want to keep us tied into. A Black woman who refuses to be pushed to the back of a bus is like a piece a' dirt that irritates the cut. A group a' boys who challenge segregation in a restaurant is another piece a' dirt. An' a young man who risks his life to get people to register to vote is one more piece a' dirt. Now, those organizations are like the puss that has to form once the dirt gets in. They're a reaction to the dirt. Part a' the process that will inevitably lead to the bursting a' that sore. Do you understand, Angel?"

"I think so, Miss Hattie. You're saying there's gonna be another big fuss, like the Southern War."

"Sorta, girl. Only, there's goin' to be some big differences. This is goin' to be a revolution that comes from the Black folks themselves. An', instead a' using guns an' bullets, they're goin' to use love an' understandin'. An' instead a' lookin' to White leaders like Mister Lincoln, we've got our own leaders right here, like Doctor King."

Miss Hattie was sayin' things that fit right in with what those two fellas had said on Friday—non-violence, love, understandin', Black leaders an' a Black revolution. But it all sounded real scary to me, all the same.

"What can we do 'bout it, Miss Hattie?" I asked, hopin' that the whole thing could jus' pass us by, so we could carry on our lives, same as always.

"First thing we can do is not to be afraid a' change, girl. Things ain't right now. They got to be put right."

I sometimes thought that Miss Hattie knew jus' what I was thinkin', an' said things to answer my thoughts instead a' my words.

"What can I do, Miss Hattie?"

"Go with it, girl. Remember, the dirt has already got in the cut, the puss is building up. It's goin' to burst. No one can stop it. So, the best thing is to move along with it. You know Angel, it's the young folks like the students who are goin' to bring the change. They aren't scared to do things. But, most a' the old folks have been bowing down so long, they've forgotten how to look up."

"I went to a SNICK meetin' with Jimmy, Miss Hattie," I blurted out, not knowin' how she'd take it.

"I know," she said quietly.

"How come?" I asked, taken off guard.

"Jimmy told me all 'bout it."

"They're gonna have a demonstration in Selma."

"I know that, too."

"What should I do, Miss Hattie?"

I wanted her to make my decision for me, but I knew her too well to think she'd let me off that easy. Yet the three words she spoke next made up my mind, not jus' 'bout that demonstration, but 'bout the whole movement.

"Remember Harriet Tubman," she said.

†††

Me an' Amie Reynolds was playing hopscotch under the shade a' the big oak tree in the schoolyard when Bernice Palmer an' three other girls came over. It was my turn, an' I was half way through my hop when I heard Bernice blurt out, "Angel Dunbar's mammy been protectin' her little baby!"

I stopped what I was doin', twisted 'round to look at Bernice, an' shot back, "What you talking 'bout Bernice?"

"Only 'bout your mama goin' 'round to tell Hattie Milton not to fill your head with fool ideas. Ask me, it's too late!"

Her an' the other three started laughin' then. I ignored their foolishness an' quizzed her for more information.

"What you know 'bout my mama an' Miss Hattie, girl?"

I demanded.

"Well, my aunty Lois was visiting Hattie Milton. They was sitting in the parlor when they seen your mother come stormin' down the pathway. She banged on the door, an' when Hattie went out there, she started yellin' at her 'bout how she was encouragin' you to get mixed up with Black agitators an' stuff. She said she was gonna keep you from her, an' Harriet oughta be ashamed a' herself."

Her words hit me like a baseball bat. I was surprised, angry, embarrassed an' sorry, all at the same time. But, of all those feelin's, it was embarrassment that was the strongest. I had to talk fast.

"An' where'd you hear that story from, Bernice Palmer?" I scoffed at her.

"From my aunty Lois' own mouth, Angel. She was there, remember?"

"You're lyin'!" I shot back.

"Then, if I'm lyin', how would I know that you went off to one a' those agitator meetin's with that brother a' yours? Your mama was yelling 'bout that, too."

I didn't know what to say next. Bernice wasn't lyin'. Mama must've really had it out with Miss Hattie. An', as if that wasn't bad enough, here was this smart little brat embarrassin' me 'bout it in front a' everyone. I felt like tacklin' that Bernice Palmer an' pummelin' her face. Instead, I spun on my heels an' started runnin'. I had to get away from all those stupid kids with their childish ways. As I ran, I felt the tears streamin' down my face. I got 'round the back a' the schoolhouse an' threw myself down. I closed my eyes. I jus' had to think. Things was gettin' so complicated. I never wanted to set Mama an' Miss Hattie off at each other. Why, what had I even done to cause that? Daddy an' Jimmy's carrying on was bad enough. Now with Mama an'

Miss Hattie, I didn't know if I could take it. An' as for Mama not lettin' me see Miss Hattie, why, that was jus' unthinkable. She was the only thing that was keepin' me from goin' crazy.

Suddenly, I felt a hand on my shoulder. I let out a surprised gasp an' twisted my head 'round. Lookin' down at me was Ronny Jackson. It was the same boy who sat at the back a' the class causin' trouble all day, but he had a look on his face like I'd never seen before. It was a look a' concern.

"Don't cry, Angel," he said. "You're face wasn't made to cry."

"What you want, Ronny?" I asked, not wantin' to let him in on my feelin's.

"I wanna talk to you, Angel, 'cause I reckon you an' me are the only two kids in this whole school can understan' each other."

"What do ya mean by that?" I forgot my own thoughts as I wondered what he was on 'bout.

"Angel," he said, wavin' his hand towards the kids in the yard, "they're still babies, worryin' 'bout their baby things. But, you an' me are different. We got bigger things on our minds, ain't we?"

"What things we got on our minds, then, Ronny Jackson?" I asked as I got to my feet.

"Things like the Black revolution, for one."

"The Black revolution?" I repeated warily.

"Yeah, Angel, the time is here, an' we're a part of it. These other kids can't even feel it but, you an' me, we're gonna be there."

"Why are you so sure I'm with you, Ronny?"

"'Cause I know what you been doing on your weekends, girl."

I stared at Ronny. He still had that concerned look on his face. He was speakin' a' things the other kids wouldn't even care 'bout. Maybe I could share my feelin's with him, after all. Anyway, it didn't hurt to try.

"You know 'bout SNICK an' Doctor King?" I asked hopefully.

"Sure, I do, girl," he said. "I know all 'bout them folks. But SNICK an' King are a waste a' time, girl—like a spit in the ol' Pacific Ocean. They ain't got no power. No, White folks got that. An', if we want it, we gotta take it. An' we ain't gonna get it from sittin' down at lunch counters."

"Ronny, it ain't 'bout power," I said, tryin' to make him see. "It's 'bout bein' equal."

"Without power we ain't never gonna be equal, girl. An' power comes from the barrel of a gun!"

Jus' then, the bell sounded out the end a' lunch. I felt relieved. Ronny was makin' me nervous with all his talk 'bout power an' guns. That weren't the way a' the Black revolution. It was to be a revolution a' love an' non-violence.

As we walked 'round to the front a' the schoolhouse, I noticed Ronny was walkin' a little taller than normal an' lookin' real proud a' hisself. It reminded me a' when he'd got everyone's attention with that argument with Mister Newton last week. The other kids stared at us as we went through the door an' made our way to our seats.

†††

For the next few weeks, things was kind a' quiet. Mama'd told me not to visit Miss Hattie no more. An' Daddy had warned me not to get involved in Jimmy's fool bidness. So, I jus' tried to keep out a' everybody's way an' not cause no trouble. Daddy an' Jimmy had sorta reached an understandin'. Jimmy wouldn't bring any a' his fool ideas into the home, an' Daddy wouldn't bother him 'bout them.

Mister Newton was learnin' us some real interestin' things in our Afro-American class. As the lessons carried on, we came to realize Black didn't have to mean dirty, ugly or sinful. Actually, we learned a new sayin', that sorta got rid a' all those bad meanings—Black is Beautiful.

Ronny Jackson was payin' more an' more attention to me. He'd always be talkin' to me when no one else was 'round, goin' on 'bout the Black revolution. The more he talked, the more I realized how different our ideas were. An' the more he spoke with me, the more he'd throw in words that showed he was interested in more than jus' sharin' his revolution ideas with me. Words like 'baby' an' 'darlin' was becomin' common. All a' his attention was a bit scary, but I liked it, jus' the same.

Anyways, Ronny came up to me one lunchtime, 'bout two weeks after our first talk behind the schoolhouse, an' he was carryin' on 'bout his Black power ideas like normal. So, I was only half listenin' when he said, " I hear those SNICK fellas are havin' another one a' those meetin's in Selma. S'pose you an' that brother a' yours are goin'?"

This was news to me, but straight away, I made up my mind to be there.

"Could be," I said, uncaringly.

"Listen, Angel, quit wastin' you're time with those SNICK fellas. All that non-violence garbage ain't gonna get nothin' but a few smashed in heads. Stay home on Friday night, baby!"

"Like I said, Ronny, could be I'll go, could be I won't."

I turned to walk away but Ronny grabbed my arm. He looked into my eyes an' said, "Please, Angel, stay home on Friday night."

I pulled away from his grip, angry at him for pesterin' me 'bout this.

"Leave me be, Ronny Jackson!" I yelled, as I ran off.

He didn't speak to me for the rest a' the week after that.

†††

When I got home that afternoon, I headed straight for Jimmy's room. I found him loungin' on his bed. When I was sure Mama couldn't hear nothin', I asked him what he knew 'bout the meetin' on Friday.

"How'd you hear 'bout that, Angel?" he demanded.

"A kid at school told me."

"Who?" he shot back.

"Ronny Jackson. He's the new kid in our class."

Jimmy got up an' closed his door then. He came back an' sat down on the edge a' his bed, next to me. He seemed real serious.

"Angel," he said, "only three people in Harpersville know 'bout that meeting—me, Peter an' Donna Reynolds. We ain't been telling no one. So how do you reckon this Jackson kid got to hear 'bout it?"

"I don't know, Jimmy!"

"What else did this Ronny kid say?"

I wondered where to start to explain to my brother 'bout all a' Ronny's crazy revolution ideas.

"Aw, he's a funny kid, Jimmy," is what I settled on sayin'. "He's got all these funny ideas 'bout fightin' against the White folks to get our freedom. He's sorta scary."

By the look on Jimmy's face, you'd think I jus' told him that Ronny Jackson was a stone cold killer or somethin'. He reached across an' grabbed my hand.

"Listen Angel," he said, real slow, "I want you to think real hard. Have you ever heard that kid say the words Black power?"

I didn't have to think hard at all.

"Only every day!" I said.

Next thing I knew, Jimmy was off that bed an' headin' for the door.

"Jimmy, where you goin'?" I called after him.

"I gotta go see Peter," he muttered as he left the room.

††‍†

I had to get to that meetin'. But it wasn't gonna be easy. Daddy wasn't jokin' when he'd warned me not to get involved. An' Jimmy had promised to Daddy that he wouldn't make me a part of it. Knowing Jimmy, he wouldn't break that promise lightly. So, how could I get there if it wasn't gonna be with Jimmy? I had to think! I muddled over it all Monday night, an' it was there, with me, at school on Tuesday, too. I was actually workin' on my divisions in algebra when an idea started comin' to me. The idea started with a name: Donna Reynolds.

Jimmy had said only him, his friend Peter an' Donna Reynolds knew 'bout that meetin' on Friday. I knew Jimmy an' Peter would go together, but they'd be too shy to invite Donna to go along with them. They both fancied her real bad, but none of 'em was game enough to say 'boo' to her. So, maybe I could go with Donna. An', if I was real careful, Jimmy wouldn't have to see me there at all.

Donna was 'bout eighteen. Her sister Amie was in my class, an' I first met Donna when I was 'round to play. I reckon that all of us girls wanted to be like Donna when we grew up. She was smart, friendly an' she dressed real nice, too. But, most of all, she was beautiful. Anyways, I made up my mind to play with Amie that lunchtime an' get myself invited over after school.

That part worked out jus' like I planned. Now, I had to figure out what I was gonna say to Donna. That afternoon, Mister Newton was gonna be readin' from *Tom Browns' Schooldays* again. He was up to chapter eight now, but it was jus' as borin' as ever. That would be the perfect time to work out my plan.

††‍†

This meeting was a far cry from the last one. For starters, when I crowded into the back seat a' Amie's daddy's car, along with her, Donna an' her older brother, John, I soon noticed we weren't headin' for Selma at all. No, we was travelin' that familiar ol' road to Birmin'ham. All the way there nobody was saying nothing, so I kept my questions to myself. When we finally got into the city, we turned off into some side streets, then came to a stop half way down a street that was full a' dirty brick houses. I couldn't see no place where a meeting could be held. As we all piled outta the car, I asked Donna where we was goin'.

"The meeting's two blocks away," she said. Before I could ask her why we didn't jus' park there, she explained that if too many cars was parked outside the meetin' place, White folks in the area might get suspicious an' that could lead to trouble.

After ten minutes a' walkin', an' no more talkin', we came to the Saint James Baptist Church. We seen some folks goin' in through the side door an', before long, we was joinin' 'em. The church was nearly full when we got in, but we managed to find some seats in the last row. I looked 'round at the folks, all squashed up in their pews. Most of the faces was old an' worn. I saw a few younger ones, an' even recognized some faces from the last meetin', but most a' the folks there that night was strangers to me.

Before long, three men came from a door behind the crowd an' walked down the aisle towards the stage. Two of 'em sat in empty seats in the front row, an' the other one made his way onto the stage. He positioned himself on the podium, looked out over the different faces before him, an' smiled. He must've been up there, jus' standin' an' smilin', for a full minute 'fore he spoke. When he did it was in a slow an' powerful voice.

"My name's Fred Shuttlesworth," he began, "and, like you folks, I live here, in the most racist city in the whole world. We've been suffering under the heat of oppression for too long, and I've got the scars to prove it. The police in this city are armed thugs, and the judges are mostly Klan sympathizers. Now, a lot of you folks know that for seven years I've been operating the Alabama Christian Movement For Human Rights. In fact, many of you have worked along with me as part of that organization. Well, what have we achieved in seven years?"

He paused then, an' spread his eyes over the crowd again, sorta like he was searching out those that'd worked in the movement with him. Then he reached onto the platform a' the podium an' grabbed hold a' his Bible. Holding it up for all to see, he continued.

"What have we achieved? Well, when I open my Holy Bible to the gospel account of Saint Mark, and read from verse two of chapter one, 'bout John the Baptist, then I see clearly what we have achieved. For, it reads, 'Look, I am sending forth my messenger before your face, who will prepare your way.'"

Again, he stopped—like he was waitin' for those words to sink into our brains. My brain was gettin' nothin' but confused. I was hopin' it would all make sense when he continued. It did, even to me.

"We've been doing a preparatory work, loosening up the soil. Getting things ready, just like John the Baptizer got the people ready for the Lord Jesus. But, what have we been getting things ready for? What lies ahead?"

He paused again, takin' 'bout half a minute to look over the crowd. He'd fix his eyes on a person, jus' long enough for them to start feelin' uncomfortable, then switch his eyes across to the other side a' the room, an' fix on a person there. When he finally spoke again, his words was softer an' quieter.

"For the past several months, I have been working with representatives of the Southern Christian Leadership Conference on the best ways to deal with the race problem in Birmingham.

After much deliberation, we have decided that a total, concerted, all-out campaign of direct action is the only answer."

Those words didn't mean much to me, but they sure got the rest a' the folks excited. From all 'round me, people was yellin' out, "Amen!" Others was clappin' their hands, an' still others was sayin' things like "'bout time," an' "sho 'nough."

After a while, the guy on the stage—Fred—put both his hands in the air, as if to tell everybody to quiet down. Then he went on to explain 'bout how the whole world was gonna see somethin' happenin' in our town over the next few weeks that was gonna make us all very proud—somethin' like Birmin'ham had never seen before. An' what we was gonna do was to break down the walls a' segregation, not jus' here in Birmin'ham, but all over the South. Now, those was words I could understan'. Excitin' words. Words that made me wanna be there—right in the middle a' what was gonna be.

Fred went on to tell us 'bout the plan him an' the Southern Christian fellas had worked out. He told us that the first target was gonna be the most hated symbol a' White racism—segregated lunch counters. Startin' tomorrow, April Third, Black folks would sit in at lunch counters across the city. From there, the movement would grow to include sit-ins at restaurants, freedom marches an' boycotts a' White stores. Then, Fred told us 'bout how the whole thing was only gonna work if it was supported by the Black community. Support was gonna come from all over the country, he'd said, but, unless the folks right here was prepared to stand up an' do it for themselves, it wasn't even worth tryin'. By now, the crowd was gettin' real excited 'bout what Fred was sayin'. The 'amens' an' 'hallelujahs' was keepin' up with every word he said.

Suddenly, the sound a' screechin' tires filled the room, an' Fred's voice an' the crowd's 'amens' became a background noise.

Next, came the sound a' breakin' glass, an' then we could hear the car takin' off. I twisted my head 'round towards the back doors. 'Bout six men, includin' Amie's daddy an' brother, was hurrying out. I looked back towards the stage to see Fred with his arms in the air, ready to calm us all down.

"Now, that's what we gotta expect from those White folks,' he yelled out,' but, we jus' gotta keep our heads. Ain't no problem here. Jus' a bit of broken glass, that's' all."

Then, Fred went right on talkin', jus' like the broken glass thing'd never even happened. But, I guess, my mind wasn't as good at blockin' it out as his. I started thinkin' 'bout a whole lotta questions an' from then on Fred's talk was lost to me. Questions came to me like who would be coward enough to do somethin' like that? An', what would cause 'em to do it? An, then, this one came to my mind—what if that thing they'd thrown at the window had've been somethin' worse than a brick or a lump a' wood? What if it had've been a bullet, or even a bomb? Suddenly, a feelin' a' hatred began to build up inside a' me. Hatred for those White cowards in that car!

I was strugglin' to keep that hatred under control when the sound of an engine an' screeching tires filled the room again. The car was back. Straight away, I looked up at Fred. He jus' kept right on talkin', like those sounds had never even happened. But, a moment later, the slammin' a' car doors came to us. An unsteady buzz came across the crowd. Fred picked up on it right off.

"Now, we all know they're out there," he said calmly, "but what we're doing here is far greater than anything a few thugs can put a halt to. And our commitment to non-violence will shame people like that."

As he said those words, he pointed outside to where the sounds of arguing was comin' to us.

"The road ahead is a road full of conflict and danger," he

continued. "Let's not fool ourselves. There's gonna be violence. There's gonna be bloodshed. There may even be murder. But that's the way it has to be. Now, let's have the discipline, right now, not to let those thugs outside interfere with our purpose for being here tonight."

Fred's voice was so calm an' unworried that it seemed to quiet down the crowd, an' they gave him their full attention again. But, my attention was gone. It'd been swallowed up by the feelin' that'd taken over me, a feelin' that I couldn't control or even fully understan'. It was a feelin' a' deep hatred for those White men outside!

†††

We was on our way home again. The trouble we was all expectin' from those fellas outside never came. Fred had got the folks attention back, an' gone on to call for volunteers for the first sit-in tomorrow. 'Bout twenty people had come forward, includin' my brother, Jimmy. Now, on the way home, I felt lucky that Jimmy hadn't spotted me in that back row. But, no matter how hard I tried, I jus' couldn't get my mind offa those White fellas in that car.

"How'd you reckon those White fellas found out 'bout the meeting?" I said, to nobody in particular.

It was Amie's daddy who answered.

"They weren't White folks, girl," he said. "Their skin was Black as your behind!"

Now, if Amie's daddy hadn't've said it so loud an' clear, I would've swore I heard him wrong. But, as it was, there was no mistakin' it. I let his words sink into my brain.

They wasn't White folks, they was Black folks!

That jus' didn't make no sense to me. Surely, Amie's daddy

had got it wrong. I had to set him right.

"But Fred said—"

"Listen, girl," he cut me off, "I went out there and I spoke to those fellas. There was four of 'em. One wasn't even much bigger than you. They was Black Muslims."

He said that last bit as if it would explain everythin' they'd done, but he might as well've said they was Martians for all the sense it made to me.

But then, Amie's brother, John, looked across the back seat at me.

"I saw those fellas too, Angel," he said. "I've seen that small kid before. I couldn't think where, but now I know. You remember a couple weeks ago when I came to pick up Amie early from school? Well, he was there, in your class. Actually, he was sitting right behind you. He's that new kid. What's his name again?"

All of a sudden, I felt ill. A tightness came over my whole body, an' my face was gettin' hot. Yet, I could feel everyone's eyes on me. It was all I could do to form the word in my mouth. When it did come out, it wasn't much more than a painful whimper.

"Ronny."

Chapter FOUR
ALABAMA, EARLY APRIL 1963

I don't remember much 'bout the trip home from Birmin'ham that night. What I do remember is that the shock a' hearin' Ronny was a part a' that trouble was causin' a poundin' in my head that felt like my brain was gonna explode. Anyways, when Donna's daddy dropped me off at our corner, I had only one thought. That thought caused me to turn away from our house, an' start runnin' the other way. Even though it was the dark a' night, that one thought took away any fear I would usually have. As I ran, I felt the sweat start rollin' down my face an' back. An achin' feelin' was buildin' up in my ribs. But, even as the sweat rolled down my forehead an' into my eyes, an' my insides screamed out for rest, I kept goin'. That one thought—to get to Miss Hattie—was so strong that I found myself flyin' down the familiar streets a' my neighborhood like a person possessed. As I sped down those empty streets, I could make out a' the darkness the landmarks a' my little world. There was the rope swing in the Anderson's yard, the dead car in the middle a' Tom Noonan's yard, an' the ancient oak tree on the corner a' Seventh an' Lincoln Avenues that Miss Hattie'd said 'd been alive for more than a hundred years. Finally, I was goin' 'round Seventh Avenue corner, an' then I was flyin' across her yard, up onto the porch, an' poundin' down her front door. As my fists banged on that door, my mind was again filled with that throbbin' pain.

Within moments, Miss Hattie's hall light flicked on.

"Who's out there?"

"Miss Hattie!"

"Angel?"

The door flung open an' I rushed into her arms. As I hugged her tight, I broke into a sobbin' cry. I was so relieved to be back in Miss Hattie's world. Her fingers matted through my hair as she whispered, "Its' all right, girl. Old Miss Hattie here now."

I pressed my face closer against her woolen night dress, an' at that moment, with the sweat coverin' my body, the tears runnin' down my face, an' the pain still throbbin' in my brain, I felt closer to that old woman than I ever been to any human bein' in my life.

"Let's sit down," she finally suggested.

We made our way into the kitchen an' I collapsed into one a' the dinin' chairs. As she went back to close the porch door, I suddenly began to feel a little foolish. Foolish to have gotten so worked up over all a' this. Foolish to be annoyin' an old woman in the middle a' the night. An' foolish to have let Ronny Jackson into my heart. For I had—jus' that little bit. When she came back an' sat across from me, I told Miss Hattie everythin' that'd happened—from how I lied to Daddy an' Mama 'bout stayin' over at Amie's place, to the things Fred talked 'bout, then the disturbance an', finally, how I found out that Ronny was mixed up in it. It felt better jus' to be able to share it all with her. The last few weeks'd been so strange not bein' able to see her. Now, I was beginnin' to feel whole again.

"You know, your mama would have a fit if she knew you'd come over here, don't you?" she asked, after soakin' in all my information.

"I know, Miss Hattie, but I jus' had to see ya!"

"So, what you gonna do 'bout all this, girl?"

"What can I do, Miss Hattie?" I asked, desperately. "I felt so much hate for those folks who smashed that window. That's when I thought they was White. Now, I know they was Black, I don't know how to feel. An', I don't know how I can face Ronny Jackson on Monday, neither."

"You'll face him all right, Angel. And not only that, but you'll treat the boy with respect."

She said that last word a little louder, like she really wanted to make it stan' out. The word caught me off guard. Respect? Why should I treat that trouble-makin' coward with respect? Miss Hattie picked up on my confusion.

"Before you judge someone," she said, "take a long, quiet walk in their shoes."

†††

I spent the rest a' that night on Miss Hattie's couch. I didn't realize how tired I was 'til my head was snuggled up against the armrest a' her big ol' chair. Right away, I was driftin' into a deep, exhausted sleep. I didn't wake 'til nearly the middle a' the day. When I did, Miss Hattie'd finished all her housework, an' was jus' fixin' to tend to the weeds in her garden. I splashed some water on my face, thanked Miss Hattie for all a' her help, an' headed for home.

I had to circle 'round two blocks to make it look like I was comin' from the direction a' the Reynolds home. But I wasn't in no hurry, so I jus' took it real slow. As I went back past the houses I'd run by last night, I thought how different they looked now. It was almost like the sunlight an' people'd breathed life into all a' those dark shapes an' now they was real. The rope swing in the Anderson's yard was the center of attention for three half naked kids. The dead car in Tom Noonan's yard had it's hood open, an' a bunch a' tools spread out before it, an' even the ancient oak tree seemed to have come to life. It was sorta like, when I passed by last night, those figures was jus' shadows in a dream. Oh, how I wished that last night had been a dream. Then, I could forget 'bout it. But, it wasn't no dream, an' on Monday I had to face up to Ronny Jackson. That thought—facin' up to Ronny—kept weighin' down on me all that mornin'. It was like a poison that slowly worked its way into all my other thoughts, destroyin' them.

Anyways, when I wandered up our yard, it seemed strangely quiet. The usual Sataday mornin' ritual a' Daddy hammerin' or sawin' somethin' on the porch, an' Mama hoein' the little vegetable garden, wasn't happenin' this day. Instead, I could see Mama through the kitchen window, but there wasn't no sign a' Daddy. I skipped over the porch an' through the front door. I made a special effort to clear my mind, so's I could tell Mama 'bout the good time I had stayin' over at the Reynolds house. I never got the chance. From the moment I saw her, I could tell somethin' was wrong with Mama. She was standin' at the sink, washin' the breakfast dishes. But, when she turned towards me, I saw pain in her eyes.

"What's wrong, Mama?" I asked, as I sat at the dinin' room table.

"Oh, Angel," she sighed.

In those two words I could almost feel the load a' whatever it was that was weighin' her down. She dropped her cloth on the bench an' slumped down at the table across from me.

"This mornin' your brother went off to Birmin'ham to get hisself involved in some sorta protest." She spoke slow an' deliberate. "Told me he expected to get arrested." Mama clenched her fist an' fixed a firm stare on me. "Girl, he ain't playin' no game now. Arrested in Birmin'ham is jus' a couple steps off bein' shot!"

Mama began to cry, then. First, a tear escaped from one eye an' trickled down her cheek. When she noticed it, she moved her hand to wipe it away. But, then another came, an' another an', before she could do anythin' 'bout it, she was outta control. As I watched my mother sobbin' before me, I started to feel guilty. Why, I'd been so caught up with my own selfish worries 'bout Ronny, I clean forgot all 'bout what Fred'd announced for today an' what it meant for Black folks. In an instant, my mind raced back to that church. I saw my brother Jimmy steppin' forward to volunteer as one a' the front line demonstrators. Then I looked across the kitchen table, into Mama's eyes. The fear I saw there touched my heart, but I knew that there was somethin' that was bigger, more important involved here than mothers worryin' for their son's well bein'. What Jimmy was involved in was gonna change history itself. But, how was I supposed to make Mama understan' that?

"Mama, Jimmy ain't doin' this by hisself," I said softly. "There's a whole lotta folks involved who know what they're doing. They'll take care a' Jimmy."

"How they gonna protect him from the police?" she demanded.

"Well, Jimmy's been tellin' me 'bout these classes he's been takin', Mama. They train folks how to protect themselves when they're gettin' attacked. I'm sure Jimmy—."

Suddenly, Mama jumped outta her chair an' hurried over to the transistor radio on top a' the fridge. She switched it on. I glanced at the clock on the wall above my head. One o'clock. Then the flickerin' voice a' the newsreader filled the room:

10:25 am, a group of approximately 25 Negroes, led by local Negro activist Fred Shuttlesworth, began marching from the Baptist Church on Sixteenth Street towards the central business district. At approximately 11:15, they arrived outside the F.W. Woolworth's Department Store and began amassing in an illegal

manner. The police moved in at around 11:30 to restore order
and several arrests were made. We will keep you informed of
future developments.

Mama switched the radio off an' slumped back into her
chair. She sighed deeply an' closed her eyes. I could tell she jus'
wanted to escape from all a' this—to be far away from the storm
that was gatherin' 'round us.

"Don't worry, Mama," I whispered. Then, rememberin'
Miss Hattie's words, I added, "This things gonna happen, but
it's gotta happen."

She didn't cut me off like I expected, so I tried to push a little
more.

"We can't stop this, Mama, so why try an' stop it? Why not
go with it?"

"You wanna know why I jus' don't go with it, girl?" Her eyes
was wide open now, an' bearin' down on me. "Don't you ever
forget that I got thirty years more a' livin' than you an' I seen
some things."

Mama's words had a hardness to them that made me feel
uneasy. As she carried on, I could feel my throat dryin' up.

"You think I like bein' a third class citizen in my own
country?" she spat out. "You think I wanna have to scrape an'
bow before folks jus' to get what I got the natural right to—to
have to say 'sir' to White trash that other White folks wouldn't
even spit on?"

"No, Mama," I said, softly.

"No, Angel. I wants my freedom real bad. But I've been
where you an' Jimmy are at. I've seen the result. It ain't gonna
solve the problem."

"But, this time it's different, Mama," I cut in.

"It's always different, Angel," she half smiled. "But you
know one thing that never changes? White folks stayin' in power

an' Black folks goin' to funerals. That ain't no different. But, girl, I'm tired a' goin' to funerals!"

"Mama, we can't jus' give up. We gotta listen to our hearts."

As I said those words, I reached my hand across to touch hers. She quickly grabbed it an' squeezed tight.

"If you could lick my heart, Angel," she said, "it'd poison you."

There was nothin' left to say.

†††

All Monday mornin', I dreaded facin' up to Ronny. Over the weekend, I thought a lot 'bout what Miss Hattie'd said, but I still wasn't sure if I could control myself when I actually saw him. So, I sorta slid into the classroom, without lookin' at anybody, an' slunk into my seat. I got my algebra textbook out an' pretended to read it. What I was really doin', a' course, was listenin' out for any noise comin' from the desk behind me—Ronny's desk. But the minutes ticked by, the bell went, an' still no Ronny. Where was he? Too ashamed to face me?

He didn't turn up all that day. I should've felt relieved, an' I sorta did. But, there was another feelin' inside a' me, too. Even after all the pain I put myself through over him—the hatred an' confusion I been feelin'—my heart still sank when I realized he wasn't gonna come to school that day. My brain was tellin' me to forget him, but, no matter how I tried, I jus' couldn't get his face outta my mind. When the other kids spoke to me at break, I found myself wishin' that Ronny was there, so we could talk 'bout grown up things, instead a' the childish rubbish they was worried 'bout. An' then, it was midafternoon—'bout the time that Mister Newton pulled out *Tom Brown's Schooldays*—that a strange idea came to me. It wasn't really an idea at all, more a question—a question that was gonna dance 'round in my mind for a long time to come: was I fallin' in love with Ronny Jackson?

†††

I was still fightin' over my feelin's for Ronny on the way home that afternoon. My mind was so confused that I decided not to walk along with Paula an' Roberta like I usually would. Their silly talk 'bout boys an' stuff was the last thing I needed to hear. So I stayed back a few minutes an' let them get on ahead a' me.

When I did set off for home, I was glad to be on my own. Maybe, now, I could make some sense of all the crazy feelin's inside a' me. My head was tellin' me that Ronny Jackson was nothin' but trouble. He was involved in somethin' dark— somethin' scary—that I didn't want no part of. But somethin' else was pullin' me towards Ronny. I guess that somethin' was my heart. Did that mean I was fallin' for him? I didn't know. I never felt like this before. Why did it all have to get so messed up?

Jus' then, my troubled thoughts was interrupted by a noise from behind me. I quickly looked 'round, an' even then, in that moment, it was Ronny that I was hopin' to see. But it wasn't Ronny. Makin' his way slowly along the sidewalk was Josiah Reeby. He had his hands in the pockets of his worn out dungarees an', when he noticed me, he looked down at the pavement. For some reason I felt a need to talk to Josiah. So, I waited for him to catch me up.

"Hi, Josiah," I said, as he got closer.

"Angel," he replied, without lookin' up.

"You're late gettin' home today," I said as I began walkin' alongside him. "You're usually the first one out the gate.'

"Ain't no hurry," he mumbled.

Talkin' with Josiah was like gettin' your tooth pulled—slow an' painful. An' you had to do all the work. At least it was one way to get my mind offa Ronny.

"What 'bout yer brothers? Don't ya gotta look after them?"

"Don't have to worry 'bout that no more," he said. "They gone."

"Gone where?" I asked in surprise.

"Adopted!" Josiah spat the word out. Then, after a pause, he added, "White folks took 'em last week."

I could tell Josiah was hurtin' real bad. Those two boys was the only thing he had.

"Oh Josiah, I'm sorry," was all I could think to say.

"Don't matter," he shot back. "Might be the best thing for those kids. Might get some chances in a White family."

"What 'bout you, Josiah?" I asked. "How you gonna get along now?"

"Same as always—only now, it's jus' me I gotta look out for."

"What 'bout your daddy?"

"He can look after hisself!"

"You sure you'll be okay?"

I was really startin' to feel worried 'bout Josiah.

"I can get along fine," he said. "Anyways, I got me a helper."

"What do ya mean?" I asked.

He looked at me for the first time, then. He seemed a bit embarrassed 'bout somethin'.

"Don't you laugh at me, Angel!"

"Ain't gonna."

Then he reached into his dungaree pocket an' pulled out a crumpled ol' piece a' paper. He handed it over to me.

"Isaiah 57:15," I read out loud. "What's this, Josiah?"

"It's a scripture, Angel. You know, the word a' the Lord."

As he spoke, I noticed Josiah was changin'. His slow, lifeless voice was becomin' more lively, more excited, an' now he was lookin' me right in the eye when he spoke.

"I read a different scripture every day. Then, I write it down, like this, an' take it everywhere with me. When I'm feelin' low or like things is too tough, I jus' get out my paper an' it reminds me that the Lord is up there, lookin' out for me, promisin' to keep me safe."

I smiled at him.

"Why did you think I'd laugh at that?" I asked.

"Dunno. Maybe thought you'd think it was sissy."

"No, Josiah," I said. "It ain't sissy."

Josiah an' me talked much easier from then on. He told me 'bout how it was his faith in the Lord that'd helped him through when his Mama died. The family that took his brothers was from way up north in Washin'ton. He reckoned they was real nice— for White folks. His daddy'd hit the bottle real bad the night the boys went away, an' he hadn't come out of it yet. But, I had the feelin' that Josiah was gonna be all right. With his faith in the Lord an' his scripture in his pocket, he was gonna be jus' fine

I was glad I walked home with Josiah. For two whole years, I spent six hours a day in the same room as him, an' never knew him. Now, in jus' ten minutes, I finally found out what made the boy with the dead eyes tick.

†††

Jimmy an' me didn't knock when we went into each other's room. Never had. So, when I got home, I barged right in on him. I wanted to hear all 'bout the demonstration on Sataday. Jimmy was lyin' on his bed, lookin' over a piece a' paper. When he saw me, he sat up, like he'd been waitin' for me.

"Took your time gettin' home," he said.

"Yeah, so what?" I shrugged.

"Got somethin' to talk to you 'bout, Angel," he said, noddin' towards the bed.

I sat down on the edge of it, wonderin' what this was all 'bout.

"Angel, you know that meetin' I went to on Friday night?"

"Yeah," I sorta stammered, sure now that he'd spotted me there.

"Well, there was a disturbance at that meetin'. An', I reckon that kid at your school was involved in it."

I breathed a sigh a' relief that he hadn't seen me. But this was jus' as bad. Since talkin' with Josiah, I'd been able to keep Ronny outta my mind, an' I figured, if I could get Jimmy to tell me 'bout the demonstration, I could keep him out of it for a while longer. An' now, here was Jimmy, bringin' him right back to the front a' my mind again! I figured I'd jus' have to skip past it as fast as I could.

"Wouldn't surprise me." I tried to sound uninterested.

"Angel," he raised his voice a little. "Listen to me. That kid is dangerous! Now, I want you to promise me something, okay?"

"What is it, Jimmy?"

"Stay away from that Ronny kid. Don't hang out with him. An' don't even think 'bout talkin' to him 'bout race matters. Can you promise me that?"

I bit my lip. What could I say? Normally, I would do anythin' to keep Jimmy happy. But this—not talkin' to Ronny—this was too much. Maybe I could get 'round it.

"Aw, he's jus' a dumb kid, Jimmy," I scoffed.

But Jimmy grabbed my arm.

"Angel, I'm serious. Stay away from that Jackson kid, all right?"

"Okay Jimmy," I blurted back, "jus' let me go."

It was the first time I ever lied to my brother, an' it made me feel a little ashamed. If only I could get this whole Ronny bidness behind us.

"Jimmy," I said, after I pulled free from his grip, "tell me 'bout the demonstration."

Jimmy sat back on the bed, with his back up against the wall.

"Okay," he said thoughtfully, "but don't let Daddy know I've been talkin' to you 'bout this."

"'Cause I won't," I replied.

Jimmy smiled at me, an' I knew everythin' was all right between us again. I lay back on his bed, an' listened to his story.

"All right. Well, let me start at the beginnin'. At that meetin' on Friday, they'd called for volunteers to be part of a demonstration the next day. Me an' Peter an' 'bout thirty others went up. We stayed behind after the meetin' an' they told us we was gonna march from the church on Sixteenth Street into the middle a' town an' up to the court house. Then they gave us some trainin' in non-violence an' they even pretended to be White folks hasslin' us, to see how we'd handle it."

"How'd that make you feel?" I cut in.

"Well, Angel, you know, I jus' tried to shut it out an' stay focused. Anyway, the organizers told us to sing freedom songs in our minds when we was gettin' abused, an' jus' to focus on the words."

"What one'd you sing?"

"'Ain't Gonna Let Nobody Turn Me Around.' I sang it in my mind the next day, too. It really did keep me focused."

"Teach it to me, Jimmy."

"Some other time, Angel," he said. "Don't you want to hear 'bout the demonstration?"

"Okay."

"Well, they ended up givin' us these Commitment Cards, an' asked us to sign them."

"What's a commitment card?" I asked.

"Well, I've still got mine. It's over there."

He pointed to the paper he'd dropped when I walked into the room. I picked it up an' began readin' through it:

I hereby pledge myself—my person and body to the non-violent movement. Therefore, I will keep the following 10 commandments. ...

I glanced over the commandments, readin' the words that caught my eye:

meditate, Jesus, love, pray, sacrifice, observe, refrain, follow, strive.

There was room at the bottom for your signature, address an' the name a' your nearest relative. Jimmy had filled these out, puttin' Mama's name down as his nearest relative. I put the paper down an' let Jimmy carry on.

"Well, the next day, me an' Peter turned up at church at the time they'd said. Most of the others was already there. We was told to go into the back a' the church an' pick out a placard each."

"What's a placard, Jimmy?" I asked.

"It's a sign with a message on it, that you carry with you."

"What'd your sign say?"

"My one said 'Give Us American Rights.' Anyways, Mister Shuttlesworth got us all together before we set off, an' told us the plan had changed. Now we was gonna march straight towards Woolworth's an' demonstrate outside of it."

"Why Woolworth's?"

"Because their lunch counter is segregated. Remember that meetin' we went to last month, when those two guys told us 'bout that first sit-in at Woolworth's in North Carolina?"

The faces a' those two guys came back to me then. The chubby, friendly guy an' the taller, more serious one. That meetin' seemed so long ago. Was it really only last month? My mind got to thinkin' 'bout all the things that'd been happenin' over the last month, an' before I knew it Ronny Jackson's face had planted itself in my head again.

"Are you listenin' to me, Angel?"

"Yes, Jimmy," I lied for the second time.

Actually, Jimmy'd talked on for some time before I managed to get my mind back on track.

"We was marchin' up an' down the street in double file. Me an' Peter was alongside each other. White folks was gatherin' along the sidewalk. They started jeerin' at us an' callin' us names."

"Is that when you started singin' that song in your head?" I asked.

"Yeah, I guess so," he replied. "Actually, you know Angel, when it was jus' a crowd a' White people all together jeerin' at us, it didn't really bother me. But, after a while, this one kid—he must've been 'bout the same age as me an' Peter—why, he came right out of the crowd an' up to me an' Peter. He started shoutin' right in our face."

"What sorta thing, Jimmy?"

"Things that civilized people wouldn't say, Angel. But after a while a' this, that kid went an' actually spat at Peter. That was the hardest part. I could see in Peter's eyes that he was close to hittin' out at that kid, so I jus' grabbed his hand while we was marchin' an' squeezed it. I reckon that gave him the message to jus' stay focused."

"I heard 'bout it on the radio news," I cut in. "They said some people got arrested. Did you?"

"No, Angel. But I came close. Nine out of our group got arrested. They was held overnight an' then released on Sunday."

"What's gonna happen now?" I asked.

"Well, Angel, Birmin'ham has been chosen as the focus a' the movement. So, what we was involved in on Saturday was jus' the start of a big campaign. Actually, they've called it Project C."

"What's the C for?"

"Confrontation."

"What's that word mean?"

"Well, Angel, it means that we gotta expect to have a few more White folks spittin' in our faces in the days to come. But, y'know something? I'm kind a' lookin' forward to it."

"Me, too," I replied.

†††

Jimmy was right when he'd said the first demonstration on that Sataday was jus' the beginnin'. The demonstrations continued every day that week, but still there was only 'bout fifty people altogether involved. Jimmy an' Peter continued to be a part of it, too. They was skippin' school jus' to walk 'round, hold up a sign an' be made fun of. When I asked Jimmy if it was right for him to skip school like that, he told me that an education without freedom is like a nail without a hammer—it ain't gonna do ya no good. But, Jimmy made me swear not to tell Daddy what he was doing, jus' the same.

Anyways, it was that Wednesday night, jus' after our dinner meal, an' Jimmy 'n me was doin' the dishes. Daddy an' Mama was in the livin' room. Daddy'd been sorta moody over dinner on account a' havin' a hard day at work, so Jimmy an' me was keepin' our voices down 'cause we didn't wanna rile him. Jimmy was whisperin' to me 'bout somethin' that'd happened on the picket line when there was a loud knock at the door. I glanced at Jimmy. He had a strange look on his face, like he already knew who it was.

"Jimmy!" Daddy's voice came through the wall.

"Yeah, I'll get it, Daddy," Jimmy said as he headed for the front door.

I heard the voice of an elderly man greetin' Jimmy. Sounded like they already knew each other. Then I heard Jimmy go into the livin' room to get Daddy. Nex' thing, Jimmy was back in the kitchen with me.

"Who is it?" I whispered to my brother.

"It's Reverend Walker from the Alabama Christian Rights Group. Wanted to see Daddy."

"What for, do ya reckon?"

"They're callin' for a boycott of all the segregated White stores, Angel. He's here to ask Daddy to support the boycott."

It took Jimmy some time to explain to me what a boycott is an' how it was gonna do any good. Once I got that straight in my head, I wondered how Daddy was gonna take to all a' this. After all, it was one thing to argue 'midst yer own family like we been doin', but when a stranger—an' a church man at that—comes to yer door an' asks for help, well, that's a different story.

Daddy an' that Reverend Walker was talkin' together in the livin' room for nearly an hour. Jimmy an' me was playin' cards in his room when we heard Daddy's boomin' voice callin' us down. As we headed down the stairs, Jimmy whispered that he hoped Reverend Walker hadn't let anythin' slip 'bout where he'd been over the last few days.

When we got into the livin' room, Daddy introduced us to Reverend Walker. Jimmy an' the Reverend acted like they was strangers. I began to figurin' out that this man before me had already worked out what was an' wasn't best to say in front a' Daddy. I looked him over. He was 'bout six foot tall, an' solidly built. He wore thick glasses an' had a long black overcoat on. Stretched out in his chair, with his big smile, he looked real comfortable there in our lounge room. I wondered why me an' Jimmy could never feel comfortable like that when we was in the same room as our Daddy.

"Reverend Walker has come here to ask us to support a boycott a' certain stores in Birmin'ham," Daddy began. "That means not goin' into those stores an' usin' our own people instead. What do you two think of that?"

I looked at Daddy, wonderin' why he was doin' this. We didn't have no say in his decisions. I stole a glance at Jimmy. I had the feelin' that he was a bit unsure 'bout this, too—not knowin' what Daddy was up to. Anyway, he jumped at the chance to give his opinion.

"I reckon it's the best thing, Daddy. The only way to get those White folks to listen is to hit them in their pockets."

"You agree, Angel?" Daddy looked at me.

"Yes, Daddy," I replied, automatically.

"That's what I figured," he said, with jus' the start of a smile. Then, lookin' at the Reverend, he continued. "All right, Mister Walker, we'll support your boycott, an', yes, I will come to your meetin' to listen to this King fella. But, I still ain't decided on this sit-in bidness."

"Will you be bringin' your family, Mister Dunbar?" The Reverend's voice was deep an' powerful.

"No, I reckon not," Daddy replied. Then, lookin' back at us, he added, "You two, get back to your room."

We did as he said.

Back in Jimmy's room, we was both quite excited 'bout what'd jus' happened. Did this mean that Daddy was startin' to change his mind 'bout the movement, startin' to come over to our side? Oh, how I hoped so. For, that would mean no more havin' to lie, no more fightin' at the dinner table, an'—most of all—no more havin' to stay away from Miss Hattie. Yes, things would be ever so much easier if Daddy would see things our way.

"Don't be too sure 'bout it," Jimmy warned me. "Daddy's probably jus' gonna go check out what sorta fool thing I'm gettin' involved with. Don't mean he's gonna go along with it."

"But Jimmy," I said, "Daddy's goin' to listen to Martin Lutha' King. I reckon he can help Daddy to understan'."

Since my talk with Miss Hattie that time, I'd heard some good things 'bout that man.

"I sure hope so, Angel," Jimmy replied, soundin' a little unsure. "Daddy's got to learn to put his past behind him. He's got to understan' that this is a new day, a new time. It's very different to what it was, you know, Angel."

"Hey, Jimmy," I looked into my brother's eyes, "what do you reckon happened to Daddy to make him so wary 'bout all a' this?"

Jimmy didn't answer me straight off. He sorta looked away, like he was hopin' I wouldn't ask that question. After a few seconds, he looked back at me. I knew he'd got his thoughts together an' was ready to let me in.

"Well, Angel, you know that time Daddy ripped his shirt off at the table?"

I nodded, feelin' a bit unsure if I really wanted to know 'bout this.

"Well, the next day, Mama told me what'd happened to Daddy to give him those scars."

"Tell me, Jimmy."

I had to know this, even if it was gonna be horrible. I had to be able to fit in this piece a' the puzzle that made up my Daddy.

"Well, I wasn't gonna tell you until you was a bit older, Angel. But I reckon it'll be okay. Might help you to understan' Daddy a bit more. Anyways, it goes back to the days when Daddy was a porter. That was back in the '50s. I was only 'bout five then, an' you, Angel, you was jus' a baby."

I curled my body up on the side of the bed, rested my head on my elbow an' let Jimmy's words carry me back.

"Anyway," he said, "back then we never had no car. An', you know, Daddy wouldn't let us take the bus."

"Why not?"

"'Cause he couldn't put up with us havin' to sit at the back. So he said if we couldn't sit where we pleased then we'd jus' have to walk to where we wanted to get.

"Anyways, there was this one day when all four of us—Daddy, Mama, me an' you—walked to the market to get the groceries. It was the middle a' summer an' it was real hot. Well, we was walkin' home from the market in that scorchin' heat. Mama was pushin' you in your stroller. She'd piled some vegetables on top of it, an' was sorta balancin' them as she pushed you. Daddy was carryin' a full bag a' groceries in each hand, an' I had a small sack a' taters to carry. After a while, we was all sweating. Then, before long—an' I can still remember this, Angel—you started crying. Mama tried to calm you down, but it wasn't no good. You was cryin' because a' the heat. Well, Daddy decided to get you somethin' to cool you down.

"Now, we jus' happened to be passin' by a gas station. That gas station had a water tap 'round back, where the White folks restroom was. So, Daddy took his 'kerchief an' went 'round back to wet it. Soon he came back an' put that wet cloth on your head, an' cooled off your face. That made you stop cryin' an' we all carried on.

"Well, Angel, we'd only got a little ways past that gas station when we heard a fuss behind us, an' looked back. We saw an old White man with a cane runnin' towards us. There was a White kid, too, 'bout ten years old, runnin' alongside him. The kid was pointin' at Daddy, yelling,

"That's the nigger, mister."

"Well, that old White man came up to Daddy an' began yellin' right into his face."

"What'd he say, Jimmy?" I asked, hardly believin' that anybody'd be fool enough to do such a thing to Daddy.

"Well, Angel, you know how White folks can talk to you like

you're a dog? That's how he talked to Daddy. He said somethin'
like, 'Boy, what you been doing, trespassin' on my property?'

"Well, Daddy jus' dropped his groceries an' looked at the
man. Angel, I can still remember how Daddy's voice sounded—
quiet, but forceful.

"'Jus' got some water for my baby,' Daddy said.

"Then you know what that old White man did? He raised up
his cane like he was gonna hit Daddy.

"'You know better than that, boy,' he screamed. 'Niggers
ain't welcome 'round here. Especially ones who creep 'round
the back a' folks places like a snake.' That old fool whipped
the cane back like he was 'bout to smash it down on Daddy's
head. 'What if there'd been a nice White girl back there, boy?
What you do then?' he smirked at Daddy. 'Reckon you would've
defiled her real bad.'"

"What'd Daddy do?" I blurted out, amazed at what I was
hearin'.

"Well, you know, Angel," Jimmy said, "that old fool was
insultin' Daddy in the baddest way. An' what made it worse,
he was humiliatin' Daddy in front a' his own family. I can still
see Daddy standin' there. He jus' clenched his fists an' looked
down at the ground. But, I could sorta feel his temper buildin'
up inside a' him. Anyway, that White man kept right on insultin'
Daddy. But, after a while he tried to bring that stick down on
Daddy's head. That's when it happened."

"What happened, Jimmy?"

"Daddy grabbed that stick right outta his hand an' threw it
across the street. Then he grabbed the old fool by the collar, an'
said, real quiet like, 'Leave us alone!'

"Daddy pushed the man back a little as he let him go, an' he
crumpled to the ground like a rag doll."

As Jimmy spoke, I pictured it all in my mind. I knew that

Daddy'd done what any man who was pushed like that would've done, an' there ain't no one who could rightly blame him. But, I also knew that the moment Daddy'd touched that White man, there was a price that had to be paid. So, as Jimmy carried on, I felt my heart begin poundin' inside a' me. I knew what was gonna come, an' I wished I could stop it. But, I couldn't, so I jus' lay there, bit my lip an' listened.

"Well, Angel, before we knew what was happenin', a crowd a' White folks had gathered 'round. That old fool was still yellin' at Daddy—this time, from the ground. Mama had you in her arms by then, an' I was clingin' to her dress.

"Four White men moved in on Daddy, an', when he saw them comin', he yelled at Mama to get us home. She obeyed, rushin' us away so we couldn't see what was happening. You know, Angel, it's strange what you think of at times like that. All I could think was that we had to leave all of our groceries, an' even your stroller, lyin' there, all sprawled over the pavement. Funny thing was, the next morning, that stroller was sittin' outside our front door, an', you know what? It was filled up with groceries. We never did find out who put it there."

"But, Jimmy, what'd they do to Daddy?" I needed to hear the rest of it.

"Well, this is the part I never knew 'bout until Mama told me last month. All I knew was that Daddy was away for two days, an' then he came home but stayed in his bed for the next couple days before returnin' to work. Turns out they dragged him back to that gas station an' put him in the back of a van. They took him into the woods, strung him up to a tree an' that old fool who started it all whipped him."

"How many times?" I don't know why I asked that, but I jus' had to know.

"Mama told me he gave him thirty lashes. Then they took off

an' jus' left him there."

"Who freed him, Jimmy?"

"Well, there was a Mister Hubbard who used to work with Daddy. Mama went to see him soon as we got home, an' he went off in his car with his two sons lookin' for Daddy. They found him after 'bout an hour. Mama said he was unconscious. Mister Hubbard tended Daddy at his place on account a' Daddy not wantin' us to see what'd happened to him, Angel."

I looked at my brother as he spoke. He had a painful look on his face, as if the thought a' Daddy, half beaten to death, but worryin' 'bout his family first, was too much for him.

"So, that's the story, Angel. Can you see now why Daddy's tryin' to protect us—that's all he's ever been tryin' to do."

"Yes, Jimmy," I sorta whimpered.

Even though I'd been lyin' comfortably on Jimmy's bed, I felt kinda exhausted after hearin' all a' this. My stomach felt like it was tied up in a knot. I wanted to run down to my Daddy an' jump into his arms, like I would with Miss Hattie. I wanted to tell him how sorry I was for what'd happened to him—how sorry I was for cryin' that day. After all, I figured, if it wasn't for me cryin', Daddy wouldn't've gone behind that gas station, an' none of it would've happened. I wanted to do these things so much, but I knew I could never do them. Whatever feelin's I felt 'bout Daddy would stay inside a' me, an' things would jus' carry on like they always had.

That's jus' the way it was.

†††

It was Monday mornin' when I finally saw him. Funny thing was, after all the thinkin' I been doin' 'bout him, my mind was actually on somethin' else when I walked into class an' saw him slouchin' at his desk.

It was Jimmy who was on my mind. I jus' knew he'd be facin' up to White folks with his placard, an' I wished I could be alongside him. Anyways, seein' Ronny sittin' there soon switched my thoughts back onto him. But, after all the thinkin' I done, I still didn't know how to react to him. How was I gonna handle it? Ignore him? Show some interest in where he'd been? Ask him outright 'bout that Friday? I still wasn't sure. So, I ended up doin' the easiest thing—I ignored him.

He didn't seem to notice me, either, but I knew it was jus' an act. Anyways, when it came to our Afro-American session at break time, Ronny stayed in with us. It was the first time he'd done that since he'd had that showdown with Mister Newton 'bout usin' violence to get our freedom. An' not only that, but he answered the most a' Mister Newton's questions. We was learnin' 'bout some a' the great Black poets. Well, when Mister Newton learned us 'bout a man called Langston Hughes, Ronny already knew all 'bout him. He even stood up an' recited a part a one a' his poems. It was called 'Lenox Avenue Mural', or somethin' like that. I tried not to, but I felt real proud a' Ronny for knowin' so much 'bout somethin' like Black poetry. Mister Newton was real impressed with his knowledge, too. An' that Ronny, why, he was grinnin' from ear-to-ear to be the center of attention again. Well, at lunchtime, it didn't take Ronny long to corner me. Actually, I purposefully sat on my own to make it easy for him.

"How'd you know all that stuff?" I spoke first.

"Learned it at my meetin's, Angel," he replied. "Learn lots a' things there."

"That your Black power meetings, I suppose."

As soon as I said that, I remembered my promise to Jimmy an' a feelin' a' guilt came over me. But, even so, I jus' couldn't help myself.

"How often you have those meetin's, anyway?"

Ronny smiled at me.

"You seem real interested in those meetin's, Angel," he said. "I reckon you wanna come along with me."

I knew he was mockin' me, but the unknowingness a' his meetin's kinda excited me. Before I knew what I was doin' I said, "Well, maybe I jus' do, Ronny Jackson."

"Friday-six o'clock," he spat out. "Meet me here."

It took me a bit to realize what I jus' agreed to, but when I did, I quickly tried to back out of it.

"I can't, Ronny. My Daddy won't let me."

"But you want to, don't ya, Angel?" he asked, starin' into my eyes.

"I don't know," I replied.

Truth was, I didn't want to go to no stupid Black power meetin'. But I did want to be with Ronny. When he was 'round me, no matter how much I tried to fight it, I felt excited. It was an excitement that made me feel good. I reckon it was like a drug that I was gettin' hooked on. A drug that I knew was no good for me. But a drug that I had to have, jus' the same.

"I know you wanna come along, Angel," Ronny said. "Don't worry. I'll find a way to get you there."

I had to change the subject.

"I know what you did last Friday night," I blurted the words out.

"Told you not to go," he shot back.

"Why'd your people do that, Ronny?" I asked.

"To wake all those church niggers up," he said, lookin' down at the ground now.

"Wake 'em up by smashin' windows. That's real clever, Ronny."

Now I was mockin' him. I could see right off that he

didn't like it.

"Come to that meetin' with me, Angel," he said, grabbin' my hand. "Then you'll understan'."

"Told you, Ronny. I can't." I pulled my hand away.

"You'll come," he said, as if there weren't no doubt 'bout it.

His cockiness made me angry, but I didn't say nothin'. For, I knew, too, that come Friday night, I'd find a way to get to be with him at that meetin'.

✝✝✝

As it turned out, gettin' away from the house that Friday was easier than I thought. Daddy's meetin' to listen to Martin Lutha' King was on that same night. After some talk, he'd decided to take Mama along with him, after all. So, when I suggested that I stay over at the Reynolds house, they both thought that was a good idea. Mama did say that Amie's folks must be gettin' sick a' me always hangin' 'round, an' that she'd have to catch up with Missus Reynolds next week to make sure I wasn't becomin' too much of a nuisance. That was gonna be a problem. But, I'd worry 'bout that later. For now, thinkin' 'bout this meetin' with Ronny was enough for me.

So there I was, back on the old schoolyard bench, waitin' for Ronny. He was late. I felt kind a' relieved, thinkin' maybe he wasn't gonna come. I didn't know what I was in for that night, an' it felt sorta scary. But, I also had the feelin' that as long as Ronny was with me, things was gonna be all right.

Anyways, after I been waitin' for some twenty minutes, a black car slowly made its way into the school parkin' lot. When I saw that car, I took a deep breath. I jus' knew that this was the same car that'd pulled up at Fred's meetin' that Friday night. Well, the back door opened an' out came Ronny Jackson. He called me over, an' next thing I was climbin' into the back seat a' that ol' car. There was three of us in the back there—me, Ronny an' a guy who looked 'bout Jimmy's age. It was real cramped, an' Ronny had his arm 'round my shoulder. The two men in the front was jokin' to each other as the car made its way outta town. After a while, they began teasin' Ronny.

"You're woman lookin' real fine tonight, Ronny boy," the driver said, as he looked me over through the rearview mirror.

"I ain't his woman," I said softly.

The driver laughed, then an' said, "The best one's always play hard to get, Ronny. But don't you worry, boy. She'll come 'round."

Ronny didn't say nothing, jus' laughed along with the others. But as he did, the arm 'round my shoulder hugged me a little closer towards him. I didn't pull away.

✝✝✝

Well, we ended up at an old farmhouse, 'bout three miles outta town. There was 'bout half a dozen cars already parked outside when we got there. We quickly made our way outta the car, an' into the house. The room we entered was full. Probably 'bout twenty people was in it. They was mainly middle-aged men. I noticed they was all dressed in dark clothin'—a kind a' uniform a' black t-shirts an' jeans. The room, itself, was full a' smoke. Coverin' one wall was a symbol painted on a large piece a' cloth—a raised arm clenched into a fist. There was nowhere to sit, so we jus' stood by the doorway. The men we'd come with was greetin' some of the others as Ronny began whisperin' to me some a' the names a' the men at the front a' the room. I never heard a' any of 'em, but Ronny spoke the names like they was real important. As I took it all in, I couldn't help feelin' outta place. Last week, at Fred's meetin', I felt comfortable. But here I felt kinda uneasy.

The only safe thing here was Ronny. So, it was fear that caused me to grab hold a' his hand an' squeeze tight. But, I guess, Ronny read somethin' else into it, 'cause the next thing I knew he had his arm 'round me an' was huggin' me close to him. I went with it, sorta hopin' I could become a part a' him, an' nobody else would notice me.

Pretty soon, a tall, skinny guy stood up at the front a' the room. He was smokin' a cigarette, an' he stood there for a few seconds, puffin' on it while he waited for the room to quiet down. When he was ready to begin, he snuffed the cigarette out in an ashtray.

"Brothers and sisters," he began, "welcome to the revolutionary vanguard."

I looked 'round the room for any other 'sisters'. I fixed my eyes on a real attractive lookin' woman who must've been in her mid-twenties. Her hair was braided, an' she, too, had on a tight fittin' black t-shirt. She was sittin' in a couch jus' in front a' the speaker. A strong lookin' guy with a bald head was huggin' her into his body. Me an' her was the only 'sisters' in the room.

"We're revolutionaries," he continued, "because we live in a country which has one of the most repressive governments in the world."

This guy's voice had a harshness to it that put me even more on edge. As I listened to his words, the feelin' a' uneasiness I had 'bout this whole thing grew.

"Democracy in America means nothin' more than the domination of the majority over the minority," he said. "That's why Black folks can cast votes all year long, but if the majority is against us, we suffer. Our children still die, our youth still suffer from malnutrition, our middle-aged people are still plagued by sickle-cell anemia, and our elderly still face unbearable poverty and hardship. There is no democracy in

America for Black people!"

He paused then, as if to give time for his words to sink in. The problems he'd talked of was real enough, but I felt worried 'bout what his way a' fixin' 'em might be.

"As revolutionaries we must be willin' to give our all to achieve our ends. We must be organized to defend our communities from racist police oppression and brutality." His voice was gettin' louder with each statement. "The second amendment to this country's constitution gives us a right to bear arms. Brothers, we must be prepared to die for our cause!" By now, he was nearly shoutin'. He stopped for a moment, castin' his eye from person to person. "You willin' to die, bro?" he asked, pointin' to the guy on the couch.

"Yeah, man," came the reply.

"The task of the revolutionary is difficult and his life is short. Even our younger brothers must be willing to be martyrs for the greater good."

I noticed that he was lookin' straight at me, now. A shiver ran up my spine.

"You ready, Ronny?" he shouted.

My head twisted towards Ronny. He was starin' right back at the speaker. As the others in the room turned to stare at him, I noticed that familiar look Ronny had when he was the center of attention.

"I'm ready, man!" Ronny proudly announced.

As those two words sounded out, I felt my grip loosenin' in his hand. I wanted to pull him away, to get him out a' that dark room an' all those scary people. But, I knew Ronny was already a part a' them. They was his family an' this was his world. It was me who was the outsider here.

So, I jus' stood there, wishin' I was someplace else. As the speaker carried on, his talk 'bout revolution, guns an' police brutality got even stronger. I tried to switch off to it, tried to imagine what was happenin' at that other meetin'—hopin' Daddy an' Mama was takin' to Doctor King's words better than I was to this fella's.

Anyways, before long this guy was handin' out some sheets a' paper. I looked down at the copy that was handed to Ronny. The headin' was '10 POINT PROGRAM'. As I looked over the points listed on the page, I remembered Jimmy's commitment card an' I couldn't help comparin' the two of 'em in my mind. I recalled how Jimmy's piece a' paper spoke a' love, non-violence an' Jesus Christ. Then I looked at point seven on the sheet in Ronny's hand:

'We want an immediate end to POLICE BRUTALITY and MURDER of Black people.

We believe we can end police brutality in our community by organizing Black self-defense groups that are dedicated to defending our Black community from racist police oppression and brutality. The second amendment to the constitution of the United States gives a right to bear arms. We, therefore, believe that all Black people should arm themselves for self-defense.'

I pulled my eyes away from the page. I knew this way would never work; it would only make things worse. I remembered Mister Newton's words that goin' down the road a' violence would be like committin' suicide an' it was then that I realized what was the real difference between us an' them, between Fred an' that guy up the front, between Ronny an' me. It was the simple difference between love an' hate.

††††

Daddy was softenin'. It was slow at first, but me an' Jimmy was able to pick up on it right off. Listenin' to Doctor King on

Friday had seemed to make him think more seriously 'bout what was goin' on. We noticed it when we was sittin' at the dinner table on Sunday evenin'.

"How'd that meetin' go, Daddy?" Jimmy asked.

"Most interestin' son," Daddy replied.

Jimmy pressed for more.

"What'd Doctor King talk 'bout?"

"He spoke 'bout lots a' things, Jimmy," Daddy said, thoughtfully, "but, I'll tell you one thing that stood out to me. He said that to really make changes here in Birmin'ham, you gotta have a crisis to bargain with." Daddy paused, as he put a forkful a' mash into his mouth. Then he pointed the fork at Jimmy an' continued. "By takin' the silent hatred we've been sufferin' under, an' puttin' it on the TV screens an' in the papers, he reckoned we could create what he called a crisis of conscience."

"What's that mean, Daddy?" I asked.

"What it means, little girl, is that if enough good people see what the bad people down here are doin', they might jus' make those bad people change their ways."

As Daddy explained this to me, the image a' him bein' whipped half to death in the backwoods came to my mind. Surely, I thought, there must be good White people who would've stopped that if they'd been able to see it.

"What do you reckon, Daddy?" Jimmy asked.

"I don't know yet, son," Daddy replied. "That Doctor King had some fine soundin' words, but we're talkin' bout Birmin'ham. That man ain't from here. I ain't sure he knows what he's got himself in for."

"It worked for him in Montgomery," Jimmy said.

Daddy put down his fork now, an' turned his head to look right at Jimmy. Watchin' him, I was expectin' his words to be sharp, so their softness surprised me.

"In Montgomery he had the people on his side, son. But, you know, I've been hearin' a lot a' people talkin' bad 'bout what he's plannin' for Birmin'ham."

This was news to me. Doctor King was here to make our lot better. Who'd be foolish enough to speak against him. Jimmy must've been thinkin' the same thing, because he asked, "What do ya mean, Daddy?"

"Folks ain't too hot 'bout this Project C a' his. Some say the timings all wrong, what with the elections goin' on. Some others reckon he should be workin' more with our own church leaders. Anyway, that Doctor King's been rufflin' a few feathers 'round here."

"Gonna give him your support, Daddy?" Jimmy asked.

"Reckon I'll jus' wait an' see for a while, boy."

"What 'bout me an' Angel?"

Jimmy was pushin' Daddy a little further with each question. I braced myself for the point when Daddy would put an end to it. But he never did. He jus' answered Jimmy's questions in the calmest, most patient way you could imagine. It was a side a' my Daddy I wasn't used to, 'cept when he'd been drinkin'. Knowin' he was clean sober now made me feel good 'bout our family for the first time in a long while.

"Son, I ain't tryin' to keep you from this jus' for the sake of it," Daddy said. "I'm jus' doin' what I reckon is best for this family. Now, you know what I've already told you. That don't bear repeatin' now. But, I reckon there ain't no harm in the two a' you goin' along to Doctor King's church meetings. But you make sure that's all it is. Got me, son?"

"Yes, Daddy," Jimmy said quickly.

I looked across at Mama then. She was starin' down at the table, slowly eatin' her food. She hadn't said a word since she'd sat down for dinner, but I could jus' tell she wasn't keen on

what Daddy'd said. It actually showed in the way she was eatin'
her food—chewin' real slow an' deliberate, clenchin' her teeth
together each time, sorta like she was takin' out her feelin's on
that food. Rememberin' back to our conversation on Sataday, I
jus' knew what she must've been thinkin'—that Daddy's words
was encouragin' us to get more involved in the movement, that
the pain that'd been a part a' her life was gonna come upon her
children, an' that there was nothin' she could do 'bout it.

✝✝✝

On the way to school on Monday mornin', I was feelin' more
mixed up than ever. It kinda felt like I was caught in a spider
web, an' every day that spider was pullin' me in a little deeper.
I wanted to pull away from that mean ol' spider, but I had no
power to get away. Yet, I knew that if I didn't make an all-out
effort to pull away, why, that ol' spider was gonna swallow me
up. The spider wasn't Ronny. No, it was the whole Black power
movement. But, it was Ronny who was drawin' me into it, an' it
was him who I had to pull away from.

That's the decision I made on my way to school that day.
An', no matter what my heart was tellin' me, I knew I had to
be strong. I had to stand up to Ronny an' tell him that whatever
mighta been with him an' me, could never be. I had to cut him
off, an' I had to do it now, before things got worse.

Well, when I walked into that schoolroom, I tried to keep
from lookin' at Ronny. Oh, I knew he was there, all right. He was
sittin' on his desk, jokin' 'round with a couple other boys. He was
laughin' away, so when I walked in, he didn't notice me right off.
I was glad a' that. I wanted to put off facin' up to him. The urge
to walk outside again an' wait for the bell to ring came over me,
but, before I could make a move, I heard Amie callin' over to

me from the other side a' the room. I began movin' towards her, hopin' to hide myself among the group a' girls gathered over there. But, I was only half way 'cross the room when I began to feel that he was watchin' me. I didn't even have to look at him to know it. The goose bumps on my arms was enough to tell me Ronny Jackson had switched his focus to me.

"Angel, what you been up to, girl?" Amie demanded as I got near her.

"What do ya mean?" I asked, not really takin' in her question.

Amie was sittin' at her desk, lookin' up at me with a smirky frown on her face. Before she could answer my question, I stole a glance towards Ronny. His eyes was beamin' down on me, like he was studyin' my every move.

"Your mother an' father saw my folks at a meetin' on Friday night, Angel," Amie said. "Only problem was you was meant to be stayin' 'round at my place."

Amie's words hit me like a slap in the face. Thoughts a' Ronny vanished from my mind, to be taken over by this new crisis.

"What'd my Mama say?" I stammered.

"Well, my mother reckoned that she was real upset with you, but that it was your Daddy who calmed her down an' told her to let him handle it."

"My Daddy?" I repeated, not knowin' what to make a' this.

If Mama an' Daddy'd already found out I been lyin' to them, how come they hadn't cornered me 'bout it yet? How come, instead, Daddy'd treated me an' Jimmy better than he had for a long time after they'd come home from that meetin', even sayin' we could go to those church meetins' by ourselves? There was somethin' strange goin' on here, an' the unknowingness of it sorta made me a little scared.

"Where you been goin' to, anyway?" Amie asked, interruptin' my thoughts.

"I'll tell ya later," I said, grateful to see Mister Newton walk into the room. It was time to head for my desk.

As I went to sit down, I kept my eyes to the floor, not wantin' to meet Ronny's stare. I quickly slid into my seat, relieved to have my back to him now. But still, I felt nervous to know that he was there, right behind me, his eyes bearin' down on me, the sound a' his breath echoin' in my ears, his very presence weighin' me down.

An', that's how it was all morning. By 9:30, my palms was actually sweatin' with nervousness. An' yet, I couldn't really understan' why. Why was the very thought a' Ronny makin' me feel so uneasy? After all, jus' las' week, when he didn't show up for school, I was feelin' at a loss. An', now that he was here, I was goin' all crazy.

What was happenin' to me? I didn't know what it was, but what I did know was that the very thought a' havin' to tell Ronny that it was finished with us made me feel like throwin' up. An' yet I did manage to tell him. By the time lunch came 'round, it'd eaten away at me so much that I jus' had to get it out. So, I cornered Ronny early on in the lunch break. I found him sittin' in the long grass 'round the back a' the school buildin' with Danny Evans an' Paul Liston. They was all crowdin' over some pictures in a magazine, but when he saw me comin', Paul snatched it up an' stuffed it under his shirt.

"See ya, Ronny," he said cheekily, as him an' Danny disappeared 'round the side a' the buildin'.

"Hi, Ronny," I said awkwardly.

Ronny got to his feet an' started towards me. He still had that hard, focused stare that I tried to avoid in class this mornin'.

"Hi, Angel," he said, grabbin' my hand an' pullin' me towards him.

"Ronny, stop it!" I squealed, as he pushed his body against

mine. But, before I could say anythin' else, his mouth was coverin' mine, an' his tongue was forcin' it's way between my lips. I pushed both hands hard against his chest an' broke free.

"Ronny Jackson, what's got into you?" I demanded, overcome by the suddenness of his actions.

"I need you girl," he said, reachin' out for my hand again. "Angel, you an' me's meant to be together. We don't have to play no games."

He was starin' into my eyes again, takin' control a' me, makin' me follow along with him.

I had to break away.

"Ronny, I can't see you no more." I blurted the words out.

Immediately, his grip relaxed in my hand.

"I really like you, Ronny," I continued, wantin' now to soften the blow, "but we're jus' too different. It won't work with us both fightin' for different sides. Can't you see that?"

He began inchin' away from me now. His eyes had moved downwards until they was focused on the ground a few feet in front a' him.

"What 'bout love?" he said softly.

"I don't know, Ronny," I sighed, wishin' I could disappear. "All I know is that I need to do this. Maybe in a few years, things'll be different. But, right now, everything's jus' too mixed up."

Ronny lifted his eyes towards me. Yet, for what seemed like forever, he didn't speak, jus' stared into my face. Finally, he did speak, choosin' his words slowly, deliberately.

"Angel," he said, "one day you will be mine."

Then he turned an' walked straight out a' the school grounds an' 'round main street corner. As I watched him go, a tear began rollin' down my cheek.

†††

Jimmy was still skippin' school to be a part a' the demonstrations. He told me the protests was buildin' up slowly. Right now they was jus' feelin' out the White leaders a' the city, or, as Jimmy put it, seein' how the White bosses would take to this uppitiness from the good niggers a' Birmin'ham. At the same time, Jimmy said, Doctor King an' others was goin' 'round to church meetin's, buildin' up support for the bigger demonstrations that was gonna follow.

So, I'd gone to a meetin' with Jimmy on Monday night at the Baptist Church on Lennox Way. We listened to a guy named Bevel talkin' 'bout what was gonna happen over the next few weeks, 'bout how we was gonna bring 'bout the things Mister Lincoln'd promised us a hundred years ago. But, instead a' killin' others to get it, the only blood that was gonna be spilled would be our own.

This guy sure excited the crowd that night, but, when I realized Doctor King wasn't gonna be there, I felt kinda let down. I'd heard so much 'bout him that I was dyin' to finally see the man.

Well, anyway, that Bevel guy did tell us that he'd organized a special meetin' for that Thursday night. It was 'specially for school students, an' he promised that Doctor King would definitely be a speaker at that meetin'. When I heard that, I squeezed Jimmy's hand. My brother looked down at me an' winked. We both knew where we'd be that Thursday night.

†††

Mister Newton had begun usin' our Afro-American sessions to teach us 'bout what was happenin' right here in Birmin'ham. He'd spent the last week takin' us through the Montgomery Bus Boycott, an' the 1954 Board a' Education decision. We learned 'bout a brand new hero that week. Her name was Rosa Parks. Now, Mister Newton was fillin' us in on all a' those organizations with the long names—SNCC an' SCLC—an' what they was preparin' for our city. Most a' the others in the class had never heard a' those outfits. They was jus' as much in the dark 'bout Doctor King an' Mister Shuttlesworth, too. Seemed like the only ones who was up on it was Amie an' me. A'course, Ronny Jackson would've known all 'bout it too. But Ronny wasn't there. He hadn't shown up since he'd walked out on me the other day.

Amie an' me started spendin' more time together from then on. Since I didn't have Ronny 'round no more, I figured she was the next best choice. I reckoned I could talk 'bout stuff with her that Paula an' Rachel an' them others wouldn't be interested in. And, anyways, it seemed lately that all those other kids was jus' too babyish for me. All their gigglin' an' jokin' 'bout boys an' stuff was startin' to get on my nerves.

Well, me an' Amie was walkin' 'round the field one lunch time, talkin' 'bout this an' that. We was sorta feelin' each other out to see if we'd get on together. We'd jus' walked past the old oak tree on the school boundary when Amie turned to look at me.

"You're changing, Angel," she said.

"What do ya mean I'm changin'?" I shot back.

"Well, I've known you for a few years, an' I ain't never known you to lie before."

Her words stopped me in my tracks. I knew I been lyin' lately—to Daddy an' Mama, to Jimmy—but, to hear the word used by someone else to describe me, now, that was hard to swallow. I turned towards Amie. Lookin' at her there, waitin' for an explanation, I almos' started cryin'. I could feel the emotions a' the last few weeks buildin' up inside a' me, ready to come gushin' out. But, instead a' cryin', I grabbed her hand, an' tried to explain.

"I know I been actin' strange lately, Amie. But strange things are happenin'. I sorta feel like, last few months, I been caught up in an adult world, but the people 'round me are still tryin' to treat me like a little child."

"You mean your folks, Angel?"

"Yeah, my folks. But, not jus' them. The whole thing. You know, I'm dyin' to get into those demonstrations, but they say I'm too young. When they gonna see I ain't a child no more, Amie?"

"I feel the same way sometimes, Angel," she admitted. "My mother still thinks I should be playin' with dolls an' stuff. Reckons I ain't mature enough to go to the meetings. Least you get to go to them."

"Yeah, I guess so."

I kinda wanted to close the subject off, before she figured what was the real reason I been actin' strange. But it was too late. For, after we'd carried on walkin' a little ways, she said,

"There's another reason you been lying, ain't there, Angel?"

"What makes you say that?" I didn't look at her.

"Angel, what's been goin' on with you an' Ronny Jackson?" she demanded, ignorin' my question.

"What you talkin' 'bout Amie Reynolds?" I tried to sound annoyed.

"Come on, Angel," she said. "The whole schools talkin' 'bout the two a' you. Now, are you all serious?"

This time she was the one who stopped in her tracks. She grabbed me, like she was forcin' me to come clean before we could carry on.

"We ain't no more," I mumbled.

"What happened?"

I looked into Amie's eyes, tryin' to see if I could open up to her. I remembered that Miss Hattie'd told me once that you can tell what's in a person's heart from the look in their eyes. In

Amie's eyes I saw a glazed intenseness, an' I decided there an'
then to tell her everything. I told her how I felt 'bout Ronny, 'bout
how I learned he was mixed up in that scuffle at Fred's church,
'bout how I'd gone to his Black power meetin' with him, how
Jimmy'd warned me offa him, an' finally 'bout how I'd broken
it off with him the other day. Goin' over it all like that, I felt the
tears buildin' up inside a' me again. But, I chose my words real
careful, makin' 'specially sure to stay away from one word in
particular. I knew that if I faced up to that word, I would make a
fool a' myself in front a' Amie. But, that Amie Reynolds wasn't
gonna make things easy for me.

"Do ya love him, Angel?" she asked.

I knew it. Jus' the sound a' that word made my eyes glaze
over, an' I felt the first tear escape down my cheek.

"A'course," I whispered, runnin' my sleeve over my eyes.

"Then go find him, girl," she spoke with a forcefulness to her
voice that wasn't there before. "You might never find real love
again in your whole life, Angel. Do you wanna grow old never
knowin' what could've been between you 'n Ronny?"

"I guess not," I stammered.

We walked over to the fence on the school boundary. As we
looked over towards Main Street, I thought 'bout my last view a'
Ronny. Where was he now, I wondered. Was he thinkin' 'bout me?

Would I ever see him again?

✝✝✝

We arrived early on Thursday, managin' to get seats up near
the front a' the church. Pretty soon the pews began fillin' up, an' by
five to seven the room was overflowin'. I glanced 'round, lookin'
for familiar faces. I saw mostly teenagers, but, now an' then, a
kid 'bout my age was squashed in-between his brother or sister.

Like Rachel Liston, who was sittin' next to her older sister Wendy. When she saw me, Rachel gave me an excited wave. I smiled, but my eyes quickly moved on through the rest a' the crowd. Probably 'bout twenty people there was familiar to me. I quickly picked out those I knew—Paully Noonan from 'round the corner, Jimmy's friend Peter Davis, Lisa Steines who was in my class las' year, an' then, sittin' off in a corner by himself, I saw the lonely figure a' my friend, Josiah Reeby. I tried to catch Josiah's eye but he was lookin' off into space, lost in his own thoughts.

Before I could find anyone else I knew, the meetin' got underway. Mister Bevel, who'd invited us here on Monday night, was standin' at the podium welcomin' us along an' thankin' us for makin' the effort to be there. With that outta the way, he got right down to the main bidness—introducin' the man we'd all come to see an' hear.

He was shorter than I thought he'd be. With all the talk 'bout him, I guess I imagined he'd be ten foot tall an' ridin' on a white horse. But the man standin' before us was'nt no superhero. Didn't look like one anyway. Actually, he was sorta pudgy, like Mister Newton, an' he seemed to be losin' his hair early. Was this the man who was gonna lead us to freedom? Well, my first vision a' him didn't exactly fill me with confidence.

An' then he spoke.

The sound a' his voice immediately took away any doubts his appearance had given me. It was simply the richest, most powerful voice I'd ever heard. It was the sound of a leader. Listenin' to him, lettin' his words soak into your mind, gave you the feelin' that things was gonna be all right—that with him at the wheel, this train was gonna get to where it was goin'.

I let Doctor King's words fill my mind, grateful to have them crowd out all my other thoughts. Pretty soon, I was caught in his spell:

"So I say to you young people tonight that the words of Jesus

1900 years ago were very serious words. He wasn't playing around when he said to love your enemies. You see, if I hit you, and you hit me and I hit you back and you hit me back and go on, you see, that goes on ad infinitum. Somewhere, somebody must have a little sense, and that's the strong person. The strong person is the person who can cut off the chain of hate, the chain of evil."

His voice seemed to increase in power as he built each sentence upon the last one. But, then he'd pause, an' his next words would be much softer, more thoughtful:

"I'm reminded of a time, a few years ago, my brother and I were driving one evening to Chattanooga, Tennessee, from Atlanta. He was driving the car. And for some reason the drivers were very discourteous that night. They didn't dim their lights; hardly any driver that passed by dimmed his lights. And I remember, very vividly, my brother A.D. looked over and in a tone of anger said, 'I know what I'm going to do. The next car that comes along here and refuses to dim the lights, I'm going to fail to dim mine and pour them on in all of their power.' And I looked at him right quick and said, 'Oh no, don't do that. There'd be too much light on this highway, and it will end up in mutual destruction for all. Somebody got to have some sense on this highway.'"

He stopped for a moment, castin' his eyes over the crowd, givin' us time to think 'bout his little story. When he spoke next, his voice had got back its power:

"Somebody must have sense enough to dim the lights, and that is the trouble, isn't it? That as all the civilizations of the world move up the highway of history, so many civilizations, having looked at other civilizations that refused to dim the lights, and they decided to refuse to dim theirs. Civilizations fail to have sense enough to dim the lights. They just keep on hating right back. And, do you know what happens to a person when

they let hatred take over?"

Again, he paused. I thought 'bout hatred an' three images came into my mind—the girl in the candy store, the ancient White man in the court house an' Ronny Jackson. Was Doctor King gonna show me that Ronny, my Ronny, was no better than those other two? I held my breath as he continued:

"When you begin hating someone, you will begin to do irrational things. You can't see straight when you hate. You can't walk straight when you hate. You can't stand straight. Your vision is distorted. There is nothing more tragic than to see an individual whose heart is filled with hate."

His short, sharp sentences had a sorta melody to 'em that seemed to infect the audience. People started shoutin' their approval after each sentence. But, not me. I was too busy takin' it all in, lettin' his words soak down into my insides, knowin' that the truth of what he was sayin' was drivin' the gap between me an' Ronny further an' further apart:

"For the person who hates, the beautiful becomes ugly, and the ugly becomes beautiful. For the person who hates, the good becomes bad and the bad becomes good. For the person who hates, the true becomes false, and the false becomes true. That's what hate does. It destroys the very personality of the hater."

I knew what else hatred destroyed. An' no matter what my heart said, no matter what Amie Reynolds said, an' no matter what that pain way down in my belly said, the truth of it was plain an' simple.

Hatred destroyed love.

Chapter FIVE
ALABAMA, SATURDAY APRIL 13, 1963

Hot an' muggy. That's what I remember most 'bout that first big protest. By 10 o'clock the sun was already at full force, beatin' down on us, takin' away a bit a' our energy, sappin' our strength. After fifteen minutes in that scorchin' heat, the sweat was already rollin' down my face, my armpits becomin' damp, an' my eyes squintin' jus' to see. Standin' there, I thought 'bout that other day, long ago, under the same burnin' sun, when Daddy'd stopped to cool the heat from offa me. Then I remembered somethin' Daddy'd told us he'd heard Doctor King say—that we needed to take the back street beatin's that'd been happenin' to Black folks an' put 'em on center stage, for the whole world to see. Well, when I looked 'round me today, I saw a bunch a' reporters with microphones an' cameras. It was then that I wished I was a real part of the protest, not jus' a bystander. Then, I figured, I could pay Daddy back for cryin' that dozen or so years ago.

But I wasn't a real part of it. I was jus' in the crowd, gathered outside a' the Sixteenth Street church. There was maybe 500 of us 'round there, stretchin' along the pavement, down to the Kelly Ingram Park. For such a big crowd, I noticed, there wasn't much noise. Maybe the heat was takin' away the energy to talk. Or, maybe we was all jus' too excited, too nervous, too unsure 'bout what was to come next.

What did come next took us all by surprise. But, thinkin'
back, it shouldn't have. We'd been preparin' for it for weeks,
strengthenin' ourselves to handle it. But there, in front of us, in
the flesh, it still made us gasp, made us question ourselves. Was
we really ready for this? For, at 'bout 10:15, four police cars,
sirens ringin', sped up the street, screechin' to a halt right outside
the church. There was three policemen in each car an', as they
got out, it seemed like they was tryin' to make as much noise as
they could—slammin' the doors an' makin' a big show a' fittin'
their clubs an' handcuffs into their belts. They took up positions
along the crowd, starin' into the faces a' those in the front lines,
pushin' an' jostlin' ones who got too close.

A policeman positioned himself a few feet from me. I looked
up into his eyes, tryin' to read what was in his heart. But, instead
a' the hatred that I was expectin' to see there, I saw fear in that
man's face. His eyes was movin' over the crowd, never stayin'
still. I could tell he was uneasy. When the sweat started rollin'
down his forehead, I knew it wasn't jus' the sun that was causin'
it. I looked at his hands. One of 'em was nervously fingerin' the
club hangin' at his side.

Suddenly, the doors a' the church flung open an' the
demonstrators poured out—first Fred Shuttlesworth an' Mister
Ab'nathy. Everyone 'round me began yellin' an' clappin' then. But
not me. I jus' looked up at that big policeman to see what he was
doin'. I noticed his eyes was kind a' dancin' from the protestors to
the crowd an' back again. His hand was clenched 'round the club
at his side now, holdin' it tight. I knew he was afraid.

Then came the rest a' the protestors—the nameless ones.
They came out in lines a' two across. I tried countin' the groups
a' two, but gave up when I got somewhere near forty. Then I saw
Jimmy. He was walkin' alongside Peter Davis. I watched Jimmy
march past me, his eyes fixed straight ahead, an' my heart began

poundin' inside a' me. Seein' the mass a' protestors, Fred, the policemen, had seemed kinda excitin' an', somehow, unreal. But now, seein' my own brother, right there in the middle of it all, puttin' himself in danger, made me see that this wasn't no game. No, this was real life, it was real people, an' it was real serious.

I decided to keep up with Jimmy to make sure he was okay. I began pushin' my way through the crowd, keepin' time with the marchers as best I could. I guess I managed to get half way to the Kelly Ingram Park when I saw a sight that froze me in my tracks. Others saw it too, an' each of 'em flinched at the sight. It was frightenin'. For there, jus' ahead of us, blockin' the entrance to the park was up to a dozen police officers who each held a leash that was strainin' to hold back a vicious, snarlin' dog. Some of the dogs was actually rearin' up on their back legs, so that the officers had to use both hands to hold 'em back.

The marchers was closin' in on the park, an' the dogs was gettin' more crazy with every forward step. I looked over the group a' marchers, to see if I could read any fear in their faces. But each face, though different, was jus' the same—eyes starin' straight ahead, jaw firmly set, head held high. From Reverend Shuttlesworth to Jimmy, right through to that last protestor, they was movin' as one.

Then from among the policemen linin' the park, a man stood forward. He could've been any White kid's grandaddy, this fella. He wore a white shirt an' tie, an' with his dark-rimmed glasses he looked like he'd be better off behind a desk at a newspaper office than here.

"As Commissioner of Public Safety of this city, I am orderin' you to disperse," he bellowed, lookin' directly at Fred Shuttlesworth.

Fred stopped marchin' then. This caused those alongside him to stop too, an' pretty soon, the whole line a' protestors was standin' still. They stood there quietly lookin' into the faces gathered against 'em. For what seemed like ages, no one spoke. The only noise was the barkin' a' those police dogs, eager to be set free.

As the heat baked down on me, I looked over at that policeman, back by the church steps. He'd been joined by another officer an' they both had their clubs drawn. They, too, was waitin' for the next move. It was that Police Chief who made it.

"This is an illegal gathering. Your refusal to disperse leaves me no option," he yelled out. As he turned to face his men, I caught the hint of a smirk on his face.

"Go!" he commanded.

A gasp went up among the crowd, as we imagined what that order might bring. But, instead a' the dogs bein' released, a dozen or so officers came forward. They approached the leadin' protestors, first Fred, then those alongside him. Each protestor was closed in on by three officers. One would force his arms behind his back an' handcuff him, while another told him he was under arrest for paradin' without a permit. Then the three of 'em would manhandle him over to a police van that was waitin' to take him away.

We watched as 'bout forty people was arrested. It was the same thing each time. Both sides well trained to carry out their roles. The officers bullyin' but professional. The protestors quiet an' respectful. Slowly the rest a' the marchers began to fall off, driftin' into the crowd. As the marchers was forced into the police vans, the crowd would clap an' yell out their appreciation. I found this strange at first, but as I thought 'bout it I realized that these people was, by sacrificin' themselves in this way, becomin' our heroes. It was as if the police solution to this problem was actually a victory for us.

As the police began to herd their dogs back into their wagons, I noticed that police chief with the thick glasses. He was standin' there, in the middle a' the street, with his hands on his hips an' a cigar in his mouth, lookin' over the crowd as they clapped their approval. The look on his face wasn't hard to read. It was a look a' disgust.

✝✝✝

Jimmy drove us to Peter's house, which was 'bout four blocks from ours. After a bit, I sorta got the feelin' they didn't want me hangin' 'round, so I told Jimmy I would walk home from there. Actually, I had no intention a' goin' home jus' yet. So, I headed in the direction of our place until I got out a' sight a' Jimmy an' Peter. Then I circled 'round the block an' headed up Seventh Street in the direction a' Miss Hattie's place.

I hadn't seen Miss Hattie for near on three weeks. After so long, I felt like I needed to get the balance back that only she could give to me. Her porch door was wide open, so, rather than knockin', I jus' yelled out to her. Seconds later, she appeared at the door. She had an apron on, an' her hands was sticky with pastry dough.

"What you doin' here, girl?" she quizzed me, wipin' her hands on the apron.

"Jus' thought I would drop in to visit," I answered, followin' her into the kitchen.

"Ain't you meant to be keeping your distance from me still?"

She sat down at the kitchen table.

"Suppose so," I shrugged as I sat across from her, "but Mama an' Daddy sorta mellowed lately, so I figured it'd be okay."

"Oh, Angel Dunbar," she said in a mockin' kinda voice, "you figured it'd be okay, did ya? Well jus' maybe your figurin'll get us both in a heap a' trouble."

She was tryin' to sound annoyed, but I knew she was only half-serious.

"Well, you're here now, girl," she sighed. "What news have you got to tell me?"

"I been into the city, Miss Hattie," I said excitedly, "watching the demonstrations. I've jus' come from there."

"Thought you might have," she smiled.

"How come you weren't there, Miss Hattie?"

"I'll be there when it counts," she replied.

Without pressin' her on what she meant by that, I went on to tell her 'bout what I seen that mornin'.

I wanted to let Miss Hattie know 'bout how proud I was a' those marchers. But it seemed that my thoughts a' the protestors was bein' crowded out by the images that'd made the deepest impact on me—the scared policeman, the barkin' dogs, an' the old White man with the dark-rimmed glasses. So, that's what I told her 'bout.

"That'd be Bull Connor," Miss Hattie'd said after I described the ol' man.

"What do ya know 'bout him, Miss Hattie?" I asked.

"I know he's one of the most racist men in the whole state a' Alabama, Angel," she said quietly. "He knows how to keep Black folks in they place."

"He didn't look too happy when we all started clappin' those who was bein' arrested."

"I bet he wasn't," Miss Hattie said, restin' her chin on her hands. "You see, Angel, that man is a law unto himself. He likes to think this is his city an' he's gonna fight to keep it the way it's always been."

"Do ya think he'll use those dogs, Miss Hattie?"

"If he's smart he won't, Angel," she answered. "But I'm

pickin' that he ain't that smart."

"Do ya reckon we'll be able to stand up to 'em if he does?"

"Angel," she said, "If Bull Connor uses his dogs against those peaceable people, he'll be doin' as much for us Black folks as Mister Lincoln did by freein' the slaves."

"What do ya mean, Miss Hattie?" I asked, surprised at how she could even compare the two a' those men.

"Well, Angel," Miss Hattie leaned back in her chair now, "see that pair a' scissors?"

Miss Hattie was in one of her story tellin' moods again. I remembered how she'd tied in gettin' a pussy sore with the Black movement last time we'd talked 'bout this sorta thing. Now I braced myself for her to fill me in on what the pair a' scissors lyin' on the table between us had to do with Mister Lincoln an' that Bull Connor fella.

"Yeah," I said.

"Well, when I first got those scissors they was sharper than my best kitchen knife. But over the years they become dull. So now, they've lost their sharpness. Makes it hard to cut through anythin'."

She was drawin' this out on purpose—tryin' my patience, teachin' me how to think.

"What's that got to do with anythin'?" I tried not to show my impatience.

"Angel, when folks are born—be they White, Black or in-between—they're born with what we call a conscience. At first, it's shiny an' new, jus' like my scissors were. So, that conscience has got a sharp edge to it. It'll prick you when you go against it, jus' as surely as those scissors would've when they was new."

She reached across an' picked up the scissors now, runnin' a finger along an edge.

"But when it becomes dull that conscience don't work too good. It ain't even gonna prick ya, unless ..."

Miss Hattie stabbed the point a' the scissors into the tip a'
her finger. As a drop a' blood oozed outta the tiny wound, she
smiled across at me.

"Unless, you do somethin' drastic to force that dulled
conscience to sit up an' take notice."

"Like maulin' innocent folks with police dogs," I finished off.

"Exactly, girl. The world's conscience, dulled as it is, won't
stand for that."

"I sure hope you're right, Miss Hattie!' But, even so, it don't
make me any less scared a' them dogs."

†††

Ronny was back. As I entered the schoolroom Monday
mornin', my mind still on Sataday's march, I jus' 'bout knocked
into him. There he was, with his little band a' followers hangin'
on his every word. He was right back where he always wanted
to be—at the center of attention. 'Bout five of 'em was crowded
'round his desk lookin' at some pictures he was showin' 'em.

I went straight to my desk, jus' in front a' his, an' began
unpackin' my homework books from my schoolbag. My plan
was to get the job done quick an' then get outta there until the
bell rang. I was jus' 'bout to head for the door when a voice from
behind me stopped me in my tracks.

"Hey, Ronny, if you wanna be alone with your woman, we'll
understan'."

As soon as Paul Liston said it, I knew he wished he could
take it back. But it was too late. I heard Ronny's chair go flyin',
an' as I spun 'round Ronny was already on top a' him. His fist
pounded into Paul's head once, then again an', as Ronny raised it
the third time, I felt myself runnin' to him, grabbin' hold a' his
arm an' beggin' him to stop. Paul managed to squeeze out from

under Ronny as he turned to face me. As if by instinct, Ronny raised his open hand to slap me.

"Stay outta my bidness, girl!" he demanded.

"Or what Ronny, you gonna hit me, too?"

I raised my chin up, challengin' him to strike me.

But instead a' slappin' my face, he grabbed me by the shoulders an' pushed me away from him.

"Jus' stay away from me," he muttered.

I lay there on the schoolroom floor for at least a minute. I was too embarrassed to move. I didn't want to have to look at anyone, to have to meet the ridicule in their eyes. Finally, Amie Reynolds came over an' helped me to my feet. We headed straight outside.

"See how much he wants you?" she said as we sat down on the grass 'round back a' the schoolhouse.

"He don't want me, Amie," I replied, wipin' my eyes with the corner a' my dress. "He's jus' dealin' with his hurt pride."

"Angel, the boy's crazy for you. Why can't you see it?"

I turned to look at Amie. I guess my eyes must have shown that I was gettin' uptight because she sorta shrunk back.

"I told ya why I can't see him no more!" I blurted the words out, hopin' they'd put an end to her questions.

"I don't get you, Angel," she sighed. "You're only hurtin' yourself by actin' like this."

"It ain't your bidness, Amie!"

I wasn't in the mood for this. Amie was an okay friend, but she had no right pokin' her nose in where it didn't belong.

"Yeah, well I guess it is none a' my bidness if you jus' think you're too good for him, little miss Angel!"

With that, she got up an' headed back inside. I knew she was jus' bitin' back at me 'cause I told her to keep outta my bidness, but her words still cut into me, jus' the same. The idea that she'd jus' planted in my brain—that I thought I was too good for Ronny—kept naggin' at me for the rest a' that day. It wasn't until home time that I finally managed to get rid of it—managed to convince myself that I was doin' the right thing for the right reason. But even that didn't make me any less miserable.

†††

Another mass meeting. They'd been havin' 'em every night since the marches began more than two weeks ago. This was the third one that I been to. Lookin' back now, they was a highlight a' the whole movement, but then I guess I sorta took 'em for granted. To hear people talkin' 'bout the very things that all Black folks carry inside but up until now never shared with others was an amazin' experience. It brought us all closer together—made us stronger. Sittin' there, listenin' to Doctor King, Mister Ab'nathy an' Fred—lettin' their words pick you up—made ya feel like it didn't matter how many dogs ol' Bull Connor had, we was still gonna win.

But this meetin' was different. Even though the Sixteenth Street Church was full to overflowin', there wasn't one adult in the crowd. Instead, the room was full a' kids, from high school seniors like Jimmy an' Peter right down to five an' six year olds, clingin' to their big brother or sister's sleeve. A message had been read out in our class by Mister Newton two days ago durin' our Afro-American class invitin' us here tonight. Lookin' 'round me, I figured that same message must've gone out to all the schools in the area, for I never seen a church so full in all my life.

It was Jim Bevel who stepped up to the podium. From his first word, I knew this night was gonna be different. There was no nice introduction. No warmin' us up for Doctor King. No wastin' time. Instead, he grabbed hold a the microphone an' spoke jus' one short, sharp word to get our attention.

"Sick!" he said.

Then he took a step back an' waited. When the mutterin' had died down, he came back to the microphone.

"This place is sick." He spat out the words, like he was ashamed to have to say 'em. "This country is sick. This state is sick. This city is sick. An', yes, that man, the chief of police, Mister Eugene Connor he is sick, too. He's infected all those other White people 'round here, an' now they're all sick as well. Yes, my friends, we're livin' in a sick place."

The crowd was silent. They must've picked up on what I noticed—that Jim Bevel was angry an' he had somethin' to say.

"But you know who else is sick? We are sick. Oh, I'm not meanin' you young people. No, I'm talkin' 'bout the older folks, the ones who have sat back for three hundred years an' let sick White people rule over them without fightin' back. In fact, most a' those folks have got so sick that they've died. That's why the Negro has been sittin' here dead in Birmin'ham, Alabama, for the last three hundred years. Well, don't you think it's 'bout time we got up an' walked a little?"

His words had an amazin' effect on us. He'd jus' told us that our own parents, our grandparents an' their grandparents was sick—that they was no good. Yet when he asked that question every voice, even mine, joined together in a boomin', "Yeah!"

He had us hooked.

"We can't sit 'round an' wait for that old Negro corpse to come back to life. We—you—the next generation, have got to get up an' do the walkin' for them. Are you ready to do that?"

Jim's boomin' voice paused long enough to allow another "Yeah" from four hundred young throats. Then he carried on to tell us that from tonight there was gonna be a shift in the movement—a shift towards us, the children. While, there'd been some progress over the last two weeks, Jim'd said, if they carried on like they was they couldn't break down the barriers to freedom. But with the children, things could be different. He explained that we didn't have no jobs for the White man to threaten us with losin', no families to support. We was already a strong community from bein' together at school. We had the energy that the older folks didn't. In short, he said, the movement needed a boost, an' we, the children, was the only ones who could give it.

He went on to talk 'bout how it was the children who'd been the key to success in Jackson, Mississippi two years ago. I listened for a few minutes, then I lost attention as I thought 'bout what this meant for us—for me. He was wantin' us—kids who spend their time playin' hopscotch—to march against those police dogs an' fire hoses. Why, I been terrified jus' standin' in the crowd the other day. Where was I gonna get the courage to do this thing?

"Now, we've been talkin' about how old a demonstrator should be." Jim had my attention again. "Should they be seventeen, or fourteen, how about twelve? Should we limit the right of children—you children—to protest against racism? Why, before you're even born, while you're still a fetus in the womb, racism has already affected you. Your mother can't get to a decent hospital. Can't afford to feed you well. Ain't got money to buy you a crib. By the time you're born, the poison of racism is already in your system."

He paused for a good half a minute then, lettin' his words sink down into our minds. "I'd like you to put up your hand if you belong to a church," he said, his voice much softer now. Nearly every hand went up.

"You've all made a very important decision already—to accept Christ as the guidin' force in your life. That's a decision

which is far more important than whether or not to march for
your own freedom. So I say to you, if you're old enough to belong
to a church, then you're old enough to act on your faith—to do
what's right. No one, not me, not Doctor King, not even your
parents have a right to stop you doin' that!"

With that, he stood back. The hundreds a' young people in the
crowd took this as their sign an' let out a great roar of approval,
followed by at least a minute's worth a' clappin'. I wondered if
they knew what we was all in for.

†††

I couldn't get to sleep that night. I had too much goin' on in my
head. The fear a' marchin' against the police dogs an' fire hoses
was jus' the start. Jim had gone on to tell us that Doctor King an'
Mister Ab'nathy was in jail, had been for nearly a week. While
he was in jail, Doctor King had read somethin' that some White
preachers'd written 'bout him. He wrote a reply to them, an' Jim
had read some of it out to us. They'd said he had no right to be in
Birmin'ham—that he was an outsider. He wrote back that he was
in Birmin'ham 'cause injustice was here. They'd said that he was
a bad man for breakin' the law. He wrote back that an unjus' law
ain't no law at all. They'd said that he was forcin' White folks to
be violent. He wrote back that you don't blame a robbed man for
causin' the thief to steal from him 'cause he had money.

All these things was goin' 'round in my head as I lay there
in the dark, with the sheet pulled over my head. But there was
somethin' even stronger than these things that was robbin' me a'
my sleep that night. I couldn't be sure. But as Jimmy, Peter an'
me jostled our way outta that church tonight, I swore I saw the
familiar back a' Ronny Jackson's head in the crowd up ahead a'
me. Ronny at one of our meetin's. It didn't make no sense. But,

then none a' this made sense. Everythin' seemed upside down.
The adults tellin' the kids that they was gonna have to do the
protestin'. Doctor King sittin' in jail. An' Ronny at our meeting.
How much crazier was this gonna get? Yet, wasn't havin' Ronny
at our meetin's the sorta thing I been prayin' for? If only he could
hear from Jim or Doctor King himself, I figured, surely he'd see
that this was the right way. In fact, this very night, durin' part
a' Jim's talk, I actually said to myself 'If only Ronny could hear
this, then he'd see.' Jim was talkin' 'bout non-violence. He told
us 'bout one time, in Jackson, Mississippi, when some crazy
White kids'd taken this Black girl an' actually tied her to the
hood a' their car with wire. Then they drove through the Black
part a' town, showin' off what they'd done. A group a' Black
boys saw this an' got real angry. Jim foun' these boys jus' as
they was settin' out to find them a White boy to kill in revenge.
He'd stood in front of 'em, he said, an' challenged 'em. Which
White boy was they gonna kill? One a' the ones who'd done this
thing. Did they have names an' addresses? What if they picked
on some innocent White person? What if it was a doctor, yeah, a
doctor who was drivin' to the Black neighborhood to help a sick
person—maybe their own Mama? What Jim'd said next was the
part I 'specially wanted Ronny to hear. For it seemed he was
jus' like those boys in Jackson who was dyin' for revenge. Their
hearts was good—they jus' needed to change their methods.

"I'm tired a' courage in the dark," Jim'd said. "All the cowards
in the world have courage in the dark. You're gonna be jus' like
them. Why don't you show your courage in the light a' day?
Why don't you take your courage—if you're that brave—an'
join me an' fight segregation? Come an' sit in with us. That takes
courage, an' we'll do it downtown in the middle a' the day when
all the cops are watching. Or does that take too much courage
for you?"

I knew that was the sorta challenge that Ronny's pride wouldn't let him back down from. He'd be thinkin' 'bout what Jim'd said, just like I was. Maybe he was even comparin' tonight to his own meetin's. I was sure he'd be able to see that our way was better. Then he could start gettin' ridda all that hatred inside a' him an' replacin' it with love. Then, maybe, just maybe, we'd have a chance. As I felt myself finally driftin' off to sleep, I began a prayer to God. I prayed that the head I caught outta the corner a' my eye comin' outta the Sixteenth Street Baptist Church tonight had really belonged to Ronny Jackson.

†††

I found myself talkin' with Josiah Reeby at mornin' break the next day. It was still hard work tryin' to get anythin' outta Josiah, him bein' so quiet 'n all. But it wasn't hard to tell that there was somethin' that was weighin' him down more than usual.

"What's wrong, Josiah?" I asked softly.

"Nothin'," he replied, starin' off into space.

"Come on Josiah, I can tell somethin's up. You can talk to me."

Since our chat that time, I reckoned that me an' Josiah had a bond. He'd shared somethin' special with me when he'd told me 'bout the scripture in his pocket, 'n I sorta figured that gave me the right to know what was troublin' him.

He turned to look at me.

"It's my pa," he said.

"Is he still drinkin'?" I asked.

"He ain't stopped, Angel." Now Josiah was lookin' down at the ground. "But after I came back from that meetin' las' night 'n told him I was gonna march against segregation, he didn't take it too well."

"Well, Josiah," I stammered, strugglin' for the right words, "that's kinda normal, ain't it?"

His head twisted towards me then 'n he pulled the shirt up on his back.

"You call this normal?" he asked.

I stole a look at his back, but within a second, I had to look away. My mind raced back to our dinner table, to that time I stared up at my Daddy's whiplashed back, 'n, jus' like then, I felt the tears wellin' up in my eyes.

"Why, Josiah?" I whispered.

"Who knows what goes on in that man's mind when the drinks got him, Angel? I guess he didn't want me bringin' more troubles to our family. Anyways, you know what he said?"

I shook my head, not sure if I wanted to know.

"Well, after he'd sobered up some, he said that if I was hell bent on marchin', then he couldn't stop me. But, he said that he'd be there watchin'. 'N, if any White man laid so much as a finger on me, he'd take to 'em with his huntin' knife."

"How could he say that after what he'd jus' done to you?" I scoffed.

"Told ya, Angel. There's no figurin' him. But he was dead serious 'bout it, I know that much."

I was lettin' those words sink into my brain, when the bell sounded out. We'd been sittin' 'round back a' the school house, 'n as I turned to get up, I saw a figure disappear 'round the side a' the buildin'. Someone'd been spyin' on us. An' I had no doubts 'bout who it was.

✝✝✝

"Remember, what you're doin' today is a great thing. Be proud, be dignified, hold your head up high." With those words

Jim Bevel began organizin' the hundreds a' children who'd turned up this mornin' in answer to his call. This was the third day a' the child marches. They began on 'D' day, Thursday, when over nine-hundred kids got arrested. I held back that day, my courage only gettin' me to the sidelines. Friday was the same. Even though it seemed a little easier to make the jump after seein' that the dogs 'n hoses had been held back on that first day, I still couldn't do it. But now, today, Sataday May 4th, here I was. Me 'n Amie Reynolds had made a pact. We'd do it together, be each other's march buddy, each other's support.

So, at nine o'clock that mornin', I found myself squashed up alongside Amie in a pew at Sixteenth Street Baptist, waitin' for what I was sure was gonna be the scariest moment a' my life. A group of 'bout fifty was 'bout to pour out a' the main entrance onto Sixteenth Street. This was meant to draw the police towards 'em, while the main group—over two hundred of us—silently made our way out the back, two-by-two, 'n marched 'round the police, headin' for downtown.

We sat there waitin' as the first group left. Within minutes the whirr a' police sirens filled the church, 'n then the unmistakable voice a' Bull Connor. He ordered the marchers to stop, but there was no reply.

"Arrest them!"

Those two words rang out loud 'n clear. Little did Mister Connor know that they was our signal, 'n next thing we was on our feet headin' out through the rear exit. With so many of us there, it took another five or so minutes before me 'n Amie spilled out onto Fourteenth Street. The light from the sun blinded me for a moment. I blinked three or four times, then looked 'round me. Those ahead of us had already stretched out as far as I could see, a solid line a' schoolchildren marchin' in twos. There was no sign a' the police. They musta' still been busy with the group 'round front. Realizin' this, I turned to Amie at my side.

"Looks like we've tricked ol' Bull Connor already," I said, surprised at how shaky my voice sounded.

"He'll catch up," she replied, grabbin' my hand. We both squeezed at the same time, smiled at each other, then looked ahead. We strode forward, keepin' step with those ahead of us. As we rounded Fourteenth Street 'n came up towards Kelly Ingram Park, I felt glad to have Amie by my side. Even though we'd had a kinda fallin' out the other day, we both knew that what we was doin' now was more important than any a' that. This was serious, 'n everythin' else in my life could wait 'til I'd done what I had to do.

The sound a' singin' soon made its way down the line. Jim had encouraged this, sayin' it was a great way to take your mind offa your fear. I thought it was a great way to let ol' Bull Connor know where we was at, too. But I guess we weren't out there to hide from him, so pretty soon I joined in 'n the words of 'Ain't Gonna Let Nobody Turn Me 'round filled the air.

We'd got to the start a' the downtown area before Bull Connor's men'd managed to group against us. But long before they arrived we'd already drawn the attention a' the local White people. They was small groups at first, runnin' alongside us, yellin' their meanest insults. But the closer we got to downtown, the larger the crowds 'n, I noticed, the more they was made up of older people. Along the way it was mainly teenage boys who'd run alongside us, provin' what men they were. But here was what looked like the parents a' those boys—women in curlers 'n men in ties. Pity they didn't have no better manners than their kids, I thought. Actually, I noticed, it was the women who was the worst of all. Standin' there, they was screamin' at us with words that woulda got me beat black 'n blue.

We tried not to look at the faces a' those people, tried to

keep our eyes lookin' straight ahead. But, every now 'n then, I stole a glance towards them. There, jus' a few feet away from me, I saw men 'n women outta control with hatred—their faces all screwed up into ugly scowls, their voices screamin' out their hate filled words. I realized then that these people could really hurt us. They was so close an' their anger was so strong, that if any of 'em had attacked us, we'd be beaten half to death 'fore anyone could do anythin' 'bout it. Yet, in the face a' this, I noticed that I wasn't afraid. My nervousness had all but left me when we'd entered into the downtown area an' now, seein' these White adults with all this unexplained hatred for school kids they'd never seen before, I could only feel one thing—pity. I remembered Doctor Kings' speech 'bout hatred 'n what it can do to the hater, 'n I felt sorry for these people—these people who thought they was so much better than us 'n yet who had been blinded by their own hatred—a hatred that was jus' as unexplainable as it was undeserved.

Up ahead of us, above the noise a' the crowd, we could hear Bull Connor's voice over a loudspeaker. But rather than orderin' his men to begin arrestin' us, he was directin' his attention to the White crowds, tellin' 'em to get back. Slowly the people began obeyin' him, edgin' back a pace or two. But it wasn't enough for ol' Bull Connor, 'n pretty soon police officers was makin' their way down the lines, usin' their clubs to push people back even more. When they'd finished the nearest bystander woulda been more than a dozen feet away. That shoulda made us feel safer, but for me, it did the opposite. I had the feelin' that ol' Bull Connor wasn't so worried 'bout the crowd harmin' us. I figured he was more interested in makin' sure they wouldn't get hurt from whatever it was he was plannin' to do to us. No sooner had this thought come to me than the sound a' barkin' dogs filled the air.

Our line a' marchers came to a standstill. Me 'n Amie strained to see what was happenin' up ahead. Through the double line that stretched on for two blocks we was able to make out the figures of a half dozen or so men facin' the front row marchers. They was wearin' long black jackets 'n they each seemed to be holdin' somethin' in their hand, but from way back there we couldn't see what. I let my eyes run back along the crowds, further away now but still as loud. It was then that I noticed there was Black folks gathered along the way also. The police had made sure to keep them well set off from the Whites, who outnumbered them by at least two to one. I looked over those folks, searchin' out any familiar faces. I was 'bout to look away when somethin' caught my eye. There, 'bout three rows back stood the one person who I knew could give me the strength to get through this. An', jus' seein' her there seemed to be enough. For in that moment a' recognizin' her, I seemed to get a rush a' power goin' through me that pushed all fear aside. Without even thinkin' bout it I called out to her.

"Miss Hattie!"

But she never heard me. My voice was drowned out by a terrible gushin' sound comin' from ahead of us. My attention went back on those men in the black coats way up front. What was in their hands was clear as ever now—fire hoses.

They'd turned on the tap of only one a' those hoses, but the noise a' that one hose was already enough to drown everythin' else out. From way back where we was, I saw the power a' that water rushin' outta the end a' that hose.

The first half dozen pairs a' marchers had dropped to the ground when they'd seen that hose goin' on. They'd gone into what Jim had called the fetal position. But I could tell that hose was still hurtin' 'em bad. The power of it, aimed full force on their backs, was enough to push them across the street 'n flyin' into the gutter. I hoped none of 'em got hit on the bare skin, 'cause those hoses was strong enough to rip the bark off a tree. They'd surely make a mess of a young Black kid's body.

Another hose came on, movin' further down the line, turnin' our nice straight line a' marchers into a twisted mass a' bodies, tossed 'bout the street like rag dolls. As they got closer to where we stood, I could make out the cuts 'n grazes that water was carvin' onto the bodies a' the kids up ahead. I saw a kid who only looked 'bout eight or nine who hadn't managed to get into the 'fetal' position in time. That hose picked her up offa her feet 'n threw her down on top a' those who was already on the ground. Someone grabbed her 'n pulled her down, coverin' her body with theirs.

By the time the third hose came into play, the word had come down the line for us to drop into position. Before goin' down, I stole a look over towards where I had spotted Miss Hattie. She was up front now, lookin' right at me. I called to her again, 'n outta all the noise 'n confusion I heard her reply.

"Remember Harriet Tubman!"

Next thing, I was on the ground, my knees tucked up to my chest 'n my hands protectin' my head.

"You okay, Angel?" I heard Amie's voice from alongside me.

"Yeah. How 'bout you?"

"I'm scared."

Her voice was shakin'. I lifted my head enough to look at Amie. She was in the same position as me, 'cept her body was heavin' up 'n down in a sobbin' cry. I reached out for her, huggin' her into my body.

"Don't worry girl," I whispered. "We'll do this together."

I knew I had to protect Amie. Without fear I looked up to see where those firemen was at. I saw one, no more than a dozen feet ahead a' me. He was controllin' the hose by himself, 'n the look on his face showed that he was gettin' some kind a' cruel pleasure outta all a' this. He had the hose poundin' into the back of a girl 'bout my age, 'n as it ripped apart her t-shirt I saw him smile. I felt my anger risin' inside a' me, 'n the thought a' jumpin' up 'n runnin' towards that fireman flashed through my mind. Instead, I lay down again, this time coverin' Amie's body completely with mine. Together we lay there 'n waited.

As I felt the first spray a' water pass over me, I tried to brace myself, to stiffen my body. I closed my eyes 'n tightened my grip on Amie. The noise a' that hose was right alongside me now.

BOOM!

It was as if a shotgun had jus' exploded inside a' me. The pain in my side was numbin' me. I bit my lip to stop from cryin' out.

Then relief. The hose was off me. I strengthened my grip on Amie, diggin' my nails into her wrists.

BOOM!

It hit me in the same spot, the left side a' my ribs. This time it stayed there, poundin' into me until I twisted to try to get some relief. Now the hose was aimed at my left arm 'n I felt my grip on Amie bein' torn away as my arm went flyin'. A terrible pain shot up 'n down my forearm.

BOOM!

The force a' my arm flyin' had spun me 'round 'n now the hose caught me full in the stomach. It threw me across the street, away from Amie. I crawled across the pavement only to be knocked back again. It was then that I realized this fireman was singlin' me out. His hose kept up its attack, pushin' me further 'n further back—closer 'n closer to the White crowds that was now cheerin' him on. After a while, I no longer felt the pain, 'cept for my arm. I jus' lay there, in the fetal position, gettin' swept back, until that fireman got bored with me. Finally the hose was offa me. I felt relieved, but only for a moment. For when I uncovered my eyes 'n looked up I found myself starin' into the faces a' half a dozen White people.

"Shoulda stayed in school, nigga girl!" screamed a middle-aged woman as she spat on me.

I was takin' in those words when a massive pain hit me in the side a' the head. My hands went there to protect me, but the pain came again. As the blood flowed down into my eyes, the pain overtook my head 'n arm 'n I prepared to die. Everythin' went black.

Chapter SIX
ALABAMA, MAY 5 1963

I woke to the sound a' my name. I was starin' into Amie's face. She had my head cradled in her arms 'n was wipin' my brow with a wet cloth.

"She's awake," Amie called out.

Two other girls came runnin' over.

"How you feeling, Angel?" a girl 'bout eighteen, who I didn't recognize, asked me.

"My arm hurts," I whispered.

"How 'bout your head?"

"No, that's okay."

I remembered the pain I felt in my head before I blacked out. I tried reachin' my hand up to feel if the side a' my head was still there. But my arm wasn't workin'. Jus' tryin' to lift it up caused me to wince.

"That arm's broken. We better fix some kinda splint," the older girl said. Her 'n the other girl went off then, in search a' somethin' they could use as a brace.

As my full sense came back to me, I was able to take in my surroundings. I was lyin' on the floor of a basketball court. Lookin' 'round, I figured that we must be in some kinda school. But it weren't like no school I ever seen before. This place was new lookin', the hoops had nets on 'em 'n in the corner I could make out some pole vaultin' gear. It could only mean one thing.

We was in a White school's gym. The place was overflowin' with Black kids, all still drippin' wet from their run in with those fire hoses.

"What we doin' here?" I asked Amie.

"Angel, we're in prison," she said, smilin' at me. "See, the real prisons got filled, so's they had nowhere else to put us."

That brought a smile to my face, too. To punish us, ol' Bull Connor'd put us in a place we'd never get to see any other time. We weren't good enough to use these facilities. But it was okay to lock us up in here. Somehow that didn't make no sense to me. Then I remembered that Jimmy'd told me once that one a' the goals a' non-violent resistance was to fill up the jails—to have so many bodies that the police didn't know what to do with us. Well, we'd certainly done that. Maybe, now we had ol' Bull Connor on the ropes. My mind took me back to the demonstration.

"How'd I survive that beatin', Amie?"

"Didn't you see that brother who saved you?"

I shook my head.

"Listen, Angel," Amie said as she ran her hand over the dried blood that'd matted into my hair, "this skinny White fella began takin' to you with his boot. It was then that I saw Hattie Milton start runnin' over to ya. But before she got there, a Black man'd got through the crowd 'n grabbed onto that White man. Before anyone could stop him, he'd pulled a knife 'n was slashin' it at that White fella."

"What happened after that?" I asked, amazed at what I was hearin'.

"Well, I think he cut that White fella twice before the crowd got that knife offa him. Then the cops came over 'n began arrestin' all a' us. They let us care for you, but we was all forced into a wagon."

"What 'bout the man with the knife?"

"Las' I saw three cops had him on the ground."

"Do ya know who he was?"

"I never seen him before," Amie replied as she began pickin' bits a' dried blood outta my hair. "But on the way over here in the police van, somebody told me who he was."

She stopped workin' on my hair now 'n looked me full in the face.

"You know that strange kid in our class?" she asked me. "That Reeby kid?"

As I nodded I felt a sinkin' feelin' inside a' me.

"Well, someone told me that guy who saved you was that Reeby kid's father."

I took a deep breath:

Josiah's father.

I noticed Josiah wasn't a part a' the march. He musta' decided against it, not wantin' to give his daddy reason to bring violence into our peaceful protest. Yet, he'd done it anyway. Not to protect his son. No, to protect me. As I lay there thinkin' bout how crazy all a' this had got, I closed my eyes. It was then that I realized how exhausted I was, 'n before long I drifted back to sleep.

†††

On Sunday afternoon they let us outta that gym prison. All mornin' we'd seen the vans pullin' up outside in the parkin' lot, bringin' more 'n more child protestors to jail. By two o'clock the gym was full to overflowin'. They simply had to let some of us out to make way for the next wave.

In a strange way, I was kinda sorry to be leavin'. The atmosphere in that place had been more like a sleepover party than a prison. Even though I couldn't move 'round much on account a' my injuries, I still made some new friends in there.

Kids was comin' up to me, congratulatin' me for what I done out on the street. One girl said that when she saw me protectin' Amie like I did, it gave her strength to put up with that firehose 'n not cry out. They talked like I was some kinda hero for doin' what I did. That made me feel good—made me feel special. An' it made that horrible pain in my arm seem worth it.

So, we filed outta that place, past the policemen who was guardin' the doors 'n out onto the playin' field. My arm'd been braced up 'n fixed in a sling that held it close to my chest. As I looked out across the field, adjustin' my eyes to the burnin' sun, I noticed twenty or thirty figures on the grass way off in the distance. At the sight of us, they got up 'n started our way. I shaded my eyes to see if I could make 'em out. Then I recognized Miss Hattie. She was half runnin' towards us, along with what I guessed musta been the families a' some a' those other kids. When I spotted her, I called out to her, then began runnin'. We met in the middle a' the field. She threw her arms 'round me, pullin' me close, squeezin' me into her belly. We hugged like that for over a minute, neither one of us wantin' to let go. I remembered back to that time I pounded down her door late at night 'n we'd hugged each other jus' like this. I felt that same safety now, that same closeness to this ol' woman. She was whisperin' in my ear.

"I'm so proud a' you, Angel," she said.

"I'm glad ya came, Miss Hattie," I replied.

"Told you I'd be there when it counted, girl," she smiled as we loosened our grip on each other 'n made our way to the edge a' the field.

We walked in silence for a while. Then, as we got outta the school grounds 'n onto the street, Miss Hattie began tellin' me 'bout how my Daddy 'n Mama was real worried 'bout me. I hadn't told 'em what I was up to yesterday. Instead, I fed 'em another lie 'bout playin' over at Amie's place.

"I went to see them, Angel."

'You did what?' I remembered how Mama'd warned Miss Hattie offa me that time.

"Last night. I had to let 'em know what'd happened to you."

"How'd they react?" I could jus' picture Mama abusin' Miss Hattie again.

"Well, like I said, they was worried 'bout you. But you know what? After we'd talked some, 'n your Daddy'd told me 'bout what he'd heard from Doctor King, he said he could see that what was happenin' here was different than in our day. An' he agreed that you'd done what was right—what he'd expect a' his child, he'd said." She looked down into my eyes now. "Actually, he was real proud of you when I told him how you'd saved that other girl."

"What 'bout Mama?" I noticed that Miss Hattie hadn't mentioned her in all a' this.

"She was worried too." I could tell Miss Hattie was searchin' for the right words. "But, you know, Angel, she don't see things quite the same. Reckons things ain't never gonna change. But you remember that advice I gave you a while back 'bout steppin' into other people's shoes?"

"Sure I do."

"Well, your mothers' had a rough time of it, girl. Ain't surprisin' she's become bitter."

"What happened to make Mama like that?" I asked.

"Angel, it ain't my place to tell you that."

"Please, Miss Hattie?" I begged her. "I need to know why Mama's so angry all the time."

Miss Hattie didn't answer for a minute. When she finally spoke, it was slow 'n deliberate.

"Her own daddy got killed Angel. Your grand-daddy."

"I know he got killed," I said.

"Did you know that he died right in your mother's lap? That she saw the whole thing?"

I didn't answer.

Miss Hattie gave me a minute to take that in before she spoke again.

"Best way for her to deal with that is to shut it out," she said. "But all a' this is bringin' it back to her."

"Poor Mama!" I whimpered.

Miss Hattie looked down at me now, grabbin' my good hand.

"Well, enough a' that," she said, squeezin' tight. "Anyway, I had a gentleman visitor this morning. I believe you know him."

"Uh huh," I said, only half payin' attention. My mind was still on Mama.

"A Mister Jackson. Believe his first name is Ronald."

I stopped dead in my tracks.

Had I heard that properly?

"What'd you jus' say, Miss Hattie?"

"You heard me, girl. Ronny Jackson came to see me this morning. 'Bout ten o'clock, in fact."

I forgot 'bout Mama completely now. Ronny? Visitin' Miss Hattie?

"What for?" I blurted out.

"For you, girl."

"What do ya mean, Miss Hattie?"

"He was real worried 'bout you, Angel. Heard that you'd been hurt. Actually, he was angry at first. Told me that he felt like goin' out and findin' that fireman who'd been pickin' on you."

"He did?" I felt that familiar excitement rushin' through me that I couldn't explain but that always came now when I thought 'bout Ronny.

"Sure he did, Angel."

We'd carried on walkin' now, still hand in hand.

"But he actually talked himself out of it. Spoke about a fella called Bevel he'd listened to."

So, it *was* Ronny at that meetin' the other night.

"What else did he say?" I wanted to know everythin'.

"That he cares for you, Angel. That he's confused. That he don't know which way to jump."

"What'd you tell him, Miss Hattie?"

"Told him that we've had too many generations a' hatred, Angel. Told him that what we need now is a bit of love."

"Did he agree with you?" I asked, the hope risin' in my voice.

"Well, sorta," she smiled.

"What'd he say?"

She looked down on me, her eyes beamin' into mine.

"Said he loved you, girl."

I felt myself blushin' then. We'd walked on for some time when I asked, "Did you like him, Miss Hattie?"

"I liked him right fine, girl," she smiled, squeezin' my hand again.

✝✝✝

When I got to school on Monday, everyone'd heard 'bout what'd happened to me. Kids who normally never spoke to me was comin' up 'n congratulatin' me on what I done. They looked at my arm, still in that bed sheet sling, wantin' to see where it was broke 'n asked me if I had stitches in my head. Throughout all a' this, Ronny'd sat back at his desk, with his arms folded, takin' it all in. He hadn't said boo to me yet.

A crowd of 'em was still gathered 'round my desk when Mister Newton walked in. As they made their way over to their seats, I noticed that Mister Newton had some newspapers in his hands. When the class'd settled down he began readin' from one of 'em.

"The shame of Birmingham," he read.

Then he passed that paper to the kid in the seat closest to him 'n picked up the next paper:

"Courageous children fight injustice."

Again he passed the paper to one a' the kids 'n picked up another. As the papers began makin' their way 'round the class, I heard my name bein' whispered by some a' the kids. Then, when one a' those papers finally got to me, I couldn't believe what I saw. For there, right under that screamin' headline, was a photograph that took up half the page. On one side a' the picture was a fireman wearin' a dark jacket with the letters B.F.D on it. In his hands, he held a hose with water gushin' across the page. On the other side a' the page, huddled up in the fetal position on the ground, the water smashin' into her was a little Black girl an' that little Black girl was me.

I looked up at the top a' the page: *The Washington Post*. Then another paper was passed to me: *The Los Angeles Times*. This time, under the words DAY OF SHAME, was four pictures— the same one a' me along with three similar ones. The picture in the bottom left caught my eye. My mind raced back to that day. I remembered that girl a' no more than eight or nine who'd been too slow to drop down. There she was, fear written all over her face, the water drillin' into her body, an arm reachin' up to pull her down.

Mister Newton passed 'round five papers in all. Then he went on to explain to us what it meant. He said what'd happened over the weekend had been a wake-up call for the nation. He said that those pictures, splashed across the country's papers, was jus' what we needed to force change. The millions a' decent people who woke up this mornin' 'n opened their paper over bacon 'n eggs would finally see what'd been goin' on down here. An' then things'd have to change. His words had a familiar ring to 'em. I remembered how Daddy'd said somethin' similar at the dinner table once, 'n how Miss Hattie'd told me how we had to force peoples' dulled consciences to sit up an' take notice. I looked back at that copy a' The Washin'ton Post, still lyin' on my desk. At that moment I felt like we could do anythin'.

✝✝✝

It was Thursday evenin' an' I was lyin' on my bed, thumbin' through Jimmy's book 'bout Mahatma Gandhi. My arm was still in the brace those two girls'd made for me when we was locked up in that school gym. So, I held the book up with jus' my good hand. I had a feelin' like I really should be readin' this book, but it was so thick, an' the words so small, that I jus' couldn't work up the appetite for it. So, I was happy to jus' flick through an' read the odd bit here an' there that caught my eye.

I jus' started readin' a bit on page 173 'bout how the Indians in South Africa decided to burn their pass cards when I heard the door slam downstairs an' Jimmy's voice echo through the house. It wasn't the way Jimmy normally sounded—all calm an' soft spoken. This voice was shaky an' high-pitched. A second later Daddy's powerful voice drowned Jimmy out.

"Calm down, boy!" he almos' yelled at my brother.

I knew somethin' was wrong—somethin' terrible. I tossed the book on my bedside table an' headed downstairs. Jimmy was sittin' at the kitchen table, an' from the stairs, I could see him shakin'. I decided to keep my distance, so I sat down on the stairs. Daddy came in from the lounge room an' sat across from Jimmy. Mama was at the sink.

"Whats' goin' on, son?" Daddy asked. I hadn't heard him sound so carin' towards Jimmy for a long while. He must've known this was serious, too.

Jimmy wiped the beads a' sweat from offa his forehead, then looked Daddy in the eyes. From where I sat, I was able to see straight into Jimmy's eyes. The look I saw was one I'd never seen before from my brother. It was the look of a scared little boy pleadin' for his Daddy to protect him.

"It's the Reeby boy, Daddy!" he finally said.

"What's happened to Josiah, Jimmy?" The words was mine. I didn't mean to speak 'em out loud an' when I did they was shaky an' nervous.

Jimmy's eyes shot up towards me, then immediately they focused on the floor in front a' him.

"'Bout half an hour ago," he said, slow an' in control now, "we cut him down from the Chester Road bridge. He'd been hangin' there for over three hours."

Jimmy's words was like thick black curtains closin' in on my mind. A feelin' a' darkness came over me as an uncontrolled, "NOOOO!" escaped from my throat.

"Get that girl to her room," Daddy ordered.

Mama was up to me in an instant. She hugged me close, then took me off to my room. By the time we got there, I had broken into a sobbin' cry.

"Hush, girl," Mama soothed me as she helped me onto my bed.

"Not Josiah, Mama," I cried, not wantin' to accept it. 'He weren't no part of this."

What Mama said next shocked me, but in a way it also helped bring me back to my senses.

"He was Black, girl. That's as far as those White animals bother to look!"

"When's it gonna end, Mama? How many more Josiah's have

to die?"

"Girl, it ain't gonna end. White folks been killin' us for no reason since slave days. That's the way it is. An' girl, don't matter how often you get your arm broke or how many a' those Doctor Kings you have marchin' 'round causin' a fuss. Ain't gonna do nothin'."

I didn't want to hear this. Not now.

"Mama," I said, "I jus' gotta get me some sleep."

"All right, girl. Try not to think 'bout what happened."

I did try—real hard. But I failed real bad. The image a' quiet, shy Josiah Reeby, the boy with the dead eyes, swingin' off a' the Chester Road bridge haunted me long into the night. Finally, somehow, I managed to drift into a troubled sleep.

✝✝✝

I woke to a touch to the side a' my face. My eyes flickered open to see Jimmy standin' over me.

"Hi, Angel," he said.

"Hi, Jimmy," I half yawned, pullin' up the sheet to cover my eyes from the light that was streamin' in through the window.

Jimmy sat on the bed beside me. He held my hand in his. "It's all right, Angel eyes," he said. I wasn't sure if he was tryin' to comfort himself or me.

"I know it is," I said. "But, Jimmy, it's so hard."

"I know, baby. Anyway, here's somethin' I wanted to show you."

He handed me a crumpled piece a' paper. I looked down at it, immediately recognizin' Josiah's messy printin'.

It simply read, JOHN 16:33

"We found it in Josiah's pocket," Jimmy explained.

"What does it say?" I asked.

"Check it for yourself," he said.

I jumped outta my bed an' went over to the shelf that had my small collection a' books. I grabbed my Bible an' flipped open to the book a' John, chapter sixteen an' verse thirty three. I quickly read it to myself then looked over at my brother.

"Read it for me, Angel," he said.

As I began to read it again a lump formed in my throat an' I had to stop half way to wipe a tear from my cheek:

"In the world you are havin' tribulation. But take courage—I have conquered the world."

Chapter SEVEN
ALABAMA, MAY 1963

Josiah's death hit me real bad. Mama let me stay home from school that next day. She'd said that I needed time to grieve. But I knew that it wasn't so much grieving that I needed. No, it was understandin' that I was cryin' out for. Even though I was right in the middle of all a' this now, I still jus' couldn't figure out where all the evil was comin' from— the evil that would drive men to string up a child for no other reason than the color a' his skin. So, after Jimmy an' me'd looked into the Bible, I'd gone back to my bed, my mind a mass a' confused thoughts. I knew thinkin' 'bout it over an' over was gonna do nothin' but bring on a headache, but I couldn't help it.

I'd been lying there for 'bout a half hour, tossin' an' turning, makin' a mess a' my bed sheet, when I realized maybe it wasn't jus' the color a' his skin that'd got Josiah killed. Maybe it had somethin' to do with Josiah's daddy. Hadn't he taken a knife to that White fella who was kicking at me? That was somethin' somebody was gonna have to pay for big time. An' with his daddy safely locked up in jail, Josiah was the obvious victim to pay for his father's sin. An' wasn't Josiah's daddy attacking that White man to protect me? I put all a' this together in my mind like a algebra equation. The answer I came out with caused me to cry out in hopeless pain—if it wasn't for me, Josiah would still be alive!

So, I lay there, goin' deeper an' deeper into depression as the day wore on. I didn't feel like doin' nothin.' Couldn't eat. Couldn't sleep. Couldn't even think 'bout Ronny Jackson. My mind was too choked up over Josiah an' the guilt a' knowin' I was involved with his death. Mama came in to see me 'bout lunch time. I told her I wasn't hungry an' she asked if I wanted to talk 'bout what'd happened. I said no, I'd be okay, even though I knew I wouldn't be. I figured Mama'd only start goin' on again 'bout how much of a waste a' time the movement was, an' I knew I couldn't handle hearin' that. So she left me there, saying I really should be gettin' up an' doin' somethin.' I told her I would. Soon.

I lay there for another hour, doin' nothin' but stare out the window. I watched a couple a' birds flittering across from our roof to the high branches of our oak tree. They seemed so happy, so free. I wished people, with all their superiority, all their wisdom, would stop an' take a lesson from these birds. I wished we could all jus' get along together in peace.

Finally, I decided I needed to do somethin' to take my mind offa all these bad thoughts. I found myself reachin' across for my Bible, still where I left it on my bedside table early this mornin.' Without thinkin', I opened it again to John, chapter sixteen, verse thirty-three. I read those words again. I let them sink down into my brain—

in the world you are having tribulation.

Who was having this tribulation, I wondered, an' what'd that word mean anyway? I figured if I could understan' what this scripture was goin' on 'bout, it'd help me to deal with this whole thing 'bout Josiah. I decided that to get the meaning of it, I would have to read the full chapter, not jus' that one verse. So I sat on my bed, crossed my legs, used my good arm to wipe the hair outta my eyes, an' began reading from the beginnin' a' the chapter.

What I read surprised me. The speaker at verse sixteen was the Lord Jesus himself. He was talkin' to his disciples. It was jus' before he was gonna get dragged away an' hung up on a pole. Thing was, he knew this was gonna happen—that folks was gonna see him like a common criminal, like a no account slave. But, even though he knew all a' this, he could still tell 'em he'd conquered the world. What'd he mean, I wondered. I knew that to conquer was to win, to beat someone at somethin.' Yet, Jesus'd been murdered, jus' like Josiah. So, who'd he beat? I was tryin' to work this out when there was a knock at my door. Mama poked her head 'round the corner.

"You got a visitor, girl," she said.

"A visitor?" Who'd be visiting me, I wondered.

"He's waitin' for ya in the living room. Get yourself fixed up 'n get down there."

"He?" I repeated. I hardly got visitors, but I never got a 'he' visitor.

"Who is it, Mama?" I demanded.

"Some boy from your school. Somethin' or other Jackson. Now get yourself lookin' decent, girl.

Ain't good manners to keep a fella waitin'."

†††

Ronny Jackson was in my house! I didn't know what to do. I looked at myself in the mirror. What a mess! My hair all tossed 'bout. My eyes puffed up from cryin.' My crumpled nightdress still hangin' from my shoulders. How could I see Ronny like this? I would die if he had to look upon me now, I thought. But Ronny'd actually come to my home. Spoke to my own mother. Was sittin' in my own lounge room. Whatever it was that'd given him the courage to do that, I knew that I needed to see him. With everythin' else that was goin' on in my mind lately, I hadn't really noticed that Ronny was changin.' Hadn't been so loud in class lately. Less talk 'bout the Black revolution. An' on Monday, when he'd jus' sat back an' watched when everyone else was crowdin' 'round me. Not like he normally was, wanting to be the center of attention. Then there was the thing 'bout him goin' to Miss Hattie last Sunday. An' now this.

So, it was feelin's a' curiosity, mixed in with that familiar excitement that got me to quickly slip into my Church dress an' run my comb through my hair. I was on my way to the bathroom to try to do somethin' 'bout my puffy eyes, when I heard Mama call out my name. "That boy'll be falling asleep by now, girl!"

"Comin'," I called back. But, I still made my way to the bathroom. There was no way I could let him know I been cryin.'

Finally, I was standin' before him. He was hunched up in Daddy's chair, an' when I came in, he studied me like I was some sorta specimen or somethin.' I spoke first. "What you doin' here?"

Ronny didn't answer straight away. Jus' kept right on lookin' at me. After a few seconds a' this he said, "Dunno. Jus' noticed you wasn't in school today, an' my feet jus' sorta led me here. Why?"

He paused for a moment.

"You want me to go?"

"I ain't sure, Ronny," I replied as I made my way to the couch. "Depends what you got to say to me."

"What ya want me to say?"

Ronny had this way a' turning every conversation into a chess game. Today, I jus' couldn't be bothered playin' along.

"Listen, Ronny, I told you last time that it wasn't gonna work," I blurted out.

"That was then," he smirked.

"So what's changed in two weeks?" I was gettin' jus' a little annoyed with this.

"Well, maybe I have," he said, almost to himself.

I looked at him then. The cockiness was gone an' I could tell that he was kinda embarrassed. I realized then that this wasn't easy for him—this comin' over to my place an' laying himself on the line like he was. An' I didn't suppose I was makin' it any easier.

"What do ya mean?" I asked, trying to sound more friendly.

"Been doin' a lot a' thinkin', Angel," he said, more in control now.

"Thinkin' 'bout you an' me, 'bout the movement, 'bout those protests you been in. Even went to one a' those meetin's a' yours."

He said that last bit as if it'd make me real proud a' him.

"And?" I said, not ready to let him in yet.

"An' I reckon that maybe what you're into ain't so stupid. Maybe, it's gonna do folks some good. Anyway, I don't reckon it's enough to come between us no more."

He shuffled his feet as he spoke, an' I could see he was nervous. What was happening here was the very thing I had been prayin' for over an' over in my mind, an' yet I didn't feel ready to accept it.

"So, in two weeks, Ronny Jackson, you've decided to come over to non-violence?"

"Didn't say that, Angel. Said it didn't have to come between us."

"Ronny, I can't be with you if you're gonna be goin' 'round smashin' windows at all the meetin's I'm at!"

"I'm not gonna do that no more, girl."

I could tell that he was gettin' annoyed.

"Why should I believe that?" The words was jus' spillin' outta my mouth now.

"Because I love you, Angel!" he stammered.

I looked over at him. He had a pained look on his face, an' I knew now it was time to stop playin' this game.

"Oh, Ronny," I sighed, "don't say that. Not unless you really mean it."

"I do."

I sat and placed my head in my hands. Somethin' came over me then, an' I found myself sliding 'cross the couch towards him. I grabbed his hand with my good one. Next thing I knew, my cheek was resting on Ronny's hand, an' I was cryin.' An' once I started, there was no holding back. I felt Ronny moving towards me, felt his arm 'round my shoulder. That close to him I could smell the sweat that I felt on his palm. I cried tears into his hand, tried to wipe them on his forearm, an' gave up as they kept comin.' Throughout all a' this he never said a word. Jus' kneeled in front a' me there with his arm 'round me. After a while, I began pullin' myself together.

"I'm sorry, Ronny," I sniffed.

"It's all right, Angel," he whispered. "I know you're hurtin.' "

He sounded so gentle when he said that, so caring. I lay my cheek back down on his palm an' let him clear away the tears with his other hand. We talked then. It was the first real talk we'd ever had. No playin' games, no fitting into a role, jus' real straight from the heart talk. I told him 'bout Josiah. Of course, he already knew that he was dead, that was the big news at school today. But I told him 'bout the Josiah I come to know. The Josiah who'd lost the only two people he'd ever been close to—his brothers. The Josiah who never knew what his Daddy was gonna do. The Josiah who loved the Lord. I told him 'bout the scripture that Josiah always carried in his pocket, an' how I couldn't figure out the meaning a' that last one they'd found on him. He told me 'bout how he'd been goin' crazy thinkin' 'bout me. How it was that craziness that'd drawn him to Jim Bevel's meeting. That he only went 'cause he knew I'd be there. But, then when he actually listened to Jim, he said, somethin'd clicked with him an' it all kinda made sense. He talked 'bout how he'd gone to see Miss Hattie, too. How he felt so worried 'bout me. So angry at those White folks. But he'd managed to use what he'd heard from Jim, he said, an' control his anger. I squeezed his hand when he told me that. I knew then that this was real. That it wasn't no far off dream. I knew that Ronny was really changin.'

He went on to tell me 'bout somethin' that'd happened at school today. 'Bout mid-afternoon, Mister Newton had gone out for 'bout half an hour, leavin' the class with some sums to do. When he came back, he had a smile all over his face. He stood in front a' the class an' announced that at 'bout lunch time a peace agreement'd been signed 'tween Doctor King an' the other Black leaders an' the White leaders a' the city. Everythin' that Doctor King'd demanded he'd got, Ronny said, from desegregatin' the lunch counters to the droppin' of all charges against the protestors.

I looked at Ronny.

We'd won. I hugged him. He was careful not to hurt my broke arm as he pressed close to me.

"We did it." I said.

He pulled back an' looked at me.

"No, Angel," he said. "You did it. You an' all those others who had the guts to do it. Not me, I didn't do it. It was you."

"But now you know, Ronny," I squeezed his hand again. "You know that this way is the right way."

"Yeah."

Ronny'd stayed until 'bout five o'clock. After 'bout an hour, Mama'd come in to see if we wanted a cold drink. I knew she was jus' snoopin' to see what was goin' on, but I wasn't worried when she saw us there, sittin' close on the couch, still holdin' hands. Pretty soon the whole world was gonna know that me an' Ronny was together.

After a while, Ronny'd told me to get my Bible. I rushed upstairs to grab it, not wantin' to be away from him for longer than I had to. Then we'd sat on the floor an' looked at John Sixteen, Thirty-Three together. He'd explained to me what the meanin' a' that verse was, an' I listened with care, like a schoolgirl who's got a crush on her teacher. He said that tribulation means trouble, fightin', problems—jus' like what us Black folks down here is goin' through. Jesus knew he'd come to the end a' his life on earth. Yet, he could look back over that thirty somethin' years an' know that never once had he given in to the workin's a' the evil one. Never had he bowed down to Satan. He'd kept his integrity, Ronny'd said. Thats how he'd conquered the world. An' now he was sayin' to his followers that even though he was goin' away, they could take courage from his example, an' conquer the world too, jus' like he did. I thought 'bout what he was sayin'.

"I reckon Josiah kind a' conquered the world, too," I said. "He sure had a lot a' reasons to give in. But he never did. Never gave up."

"Jus' like the Lord," Ronny finished. "An' jus' like the Lord, maybe Josiah was teachin' us somethin', too."

"What do ya reckon that was, Ronny?"

"Well, I reckon he's saying to us that he never compromised, right up to his death. He remained strong. He conquered. So, when we're feelin' like we can't go on, like it's all too tough for us, remember him an' draw strength outta what he did."

"Then his death won't be for nothin'," I added.

Jus' then I heard Jimmy's voice echoin' through the house. I looked at Ronny an' began to panic. I wasn't sure what Jimmy'd do if he knew that the very kid he'd warned me away from, the troublemaker who'd been part a' that fuss at Fred's meetin' that time, was sittin' on our own livin' room floor alone with me.

I could hear Mama say "Jackson," 'n then from Jimmy a loud "What!" I decided it was time for Ronny to go.

"Meet me tomorrow, "he whispered as we made our way to the back door.

"Where?"

"At the school parkin' lot, nine o'clock."

An' then he was gone.

†††

"What are you doin', Angel?" Jimmy demanded.

I gone back upstairs after Ronny'd left, to make my bed. I only jus' managed to pull back the sheets when Jimmy'd burst in. He didn't waste any time gettin' to the point.

"You know I told you to stay away from that kid."

"That kid has a name." I didn't bother lookin' at him.

"Angel!" He was nearly shoutin' now. "He's trouble. Now if you want to be treated like an adult, you better start listenin' when your'e told things."

I turned to face him then.

"Jimmy," I said, as softly as I could, "Ronny's changed. He came to our meetin' the other day. He's okay now."

"How stupid are you, girl?" Jimmy's anger was beginnin' to frighten me. "Of course he hasn't changed. I'll bet he came to that meeting to do some sorta spying for those Black power fools. They've probably got him to target you as a way of infiltratin' into our movement. He's probably—"

"Don't be ridiculous, Jimmy," I cut him off. "Ronny loves me!"

"Oh, my goodness, Angel," he sighed. "You're thirteen years old. What do you know 'bout love?"

"I know how to listen to my heart, Jimmy," I snapped back at him.

"Now, if you've come in here to tell me to stay away from Ronny, the answer's no. So, if that's all, will you get outta my room!"

He slammed the door on his way out, an' I could hear Mama cussin' him from downstairs. I slumped down onto my bed an' gazed out the window. I saw what looked like those same two birds from earlier in the day. They was chirpin' away still, without a care in the world. I wondered why folks had to make such a complicated fuss outta everythin'.

†††

I wanted to be outta the house early the next morning, 'fore anyone else got up. But, when I tiptoed down the stairs 'bout seven o'clock, I could hear Mama already cookin' eggs in the kitchen. I told her I needed to go for a walk. She asked if I was goin' to see that boy. I said that I might bump into him later. She'd sat me down then, an' given me this talk 'bout what it was like when her an' Daddy'd met. How she was jus' gettin' over her own Daddy's death when this handsome, strong fella came on the scene. He'd been able to get her mind offa her problems, she'd said. But it took her a long while to reckon if she was attracted to him 'cause she needed him to help her cope, or if it was 'cause she loved him.

"How'd you figure that out, Mama?" I asked, amazed at how similar her story sounded to what I was goin' through with Ronny.

"Well, girl, your brother Jimmy came 'long 'n that was the end of it. Didn't matter if it was needin' or lovin' then. But, you know what? What started as a need grew into love."

She reached out to grab hold a' my good hand then, an' holdin' it in hers, she added, "All I'm sayin' to ya, Angel, is don't let your heart take you somewhere that your head don't wanna go. See, me 'n your Daddy was lucky. Could easily've been that it wasn't love, 'n that it could never've grown into love. Then we'd a' been thrown together in a life a' misery, jus' goin' through the motions."

"So, Mama, how do I know if it's love?" I looked up at her, thinkin' that this was the closest the two of us had been for a long while.

"Angel," she smiled, "you're still a child. You gotta live some before you can love. Now, I ain't tryin' to make fun a' you 'n that boy who came over yestaday. Seems like a nice enough fella. But, girl, don't mean he's gonna be the one."

She must've seen my face drop then, because she tightened her grip on my hand.

"Glory, girl," she continued, "I was five years older'n you when I first met your Daddy. Now, I hope you 'n that Ronny boy can be happy. But, don't think that it has to be forever. To an' girl ..." Her voice'd changed now. It was more serious.

"Yes, Mama."

"You learn from me. Like I jus' told you, havin' Jimmy like I did was a mighty big risk. If it hadn't worked out with your Daddy 'n me, I woulda been in a real fix. Don't you get yourself in that position. You understan' me?"

"I guess so, Mama."

That was the closest I ever got to a talk 'bout the birds an' the bees. But I was grateful to Mama for that little chat of ours that mornin'. I realized then that she understood what I was goin' through far more than I'd ever known. Because she'd already gone there.

✝✝✝

I wound up sittin' on the same old school bench that I waited for Ronny on the last time we'd arranged to get together. I didn't mind waitin'—gave me a chance to think things over. Sure, I been goin' outta my mind with thinkin' since the news 'bout Josiah. But, since Ronny's visit yestaday, things'd started to look up again. An', even though my brother wasn't too happy with me, an' Mama thought it was jus' a passin' thing, I knew that I could be happy again.

So, my thoughts went beyond Josiah. They went to the future, to the way things was gonna be now because a' the success a' the movement. An' to the way me an' Ronny was gonna be now. Yeah, I was happy to sit an' think 'bout those things. I was caught up in the middle a' day-dreamin' 'bout the two of us when somethin' grabbed at me from behind. I gasped in shock as a hand covered my eyes an' another closed over my mouth. In an instant, Josiah's face was in my mind again. This must've been what they'd done to him, I thought. Well, they ain't gonna do it to me! I bit down on the hand.

Next thing I heard a pained "Ow!" an' then Ronny was sittin' beside me, holding an injured hand in his other palm.

"Ronny!' I was angry an' relieved at the same time.

'Didn't have to bite me!' he scowled.

'Ronny, you scared me," I said, "Don't do that to me again."

"Don't worry," he replied. "Ain't too keen on gettin' my hand bit off."

"Let me have a look at it," I ordered, startin' to calm down.

I examined his hand, smiling at the teeth marks I jus' made in his first two fingers. I didn't see any blood.

"Serves you right," I said, lettin' the hand drop. "Anyway, I reckon you'll live."

"Been here long?" he asked sheepishly

"Since before eight o'clock."

"Didn't realize you was that desperate to see me."

"Wasn't," I lied. "I was jus' sick a' fightin' with my brother, so I thought I'd get outta the house before he got up." It wasn't a total lie. Me an' Jimmy hardly ever had rows, so, when we did, like yestaday, it messed me all up. That was part a' the reason I wanted to get out so early this mornin'.

"What happened with you an' him after I left?" Ronny asked.

I cupped my chin in my hands, resting my elbows on my knees. I tried to explain to him 'bout me an' Jimmy. As I did, I remembered not so long ago strugglin' to explain to Jimmy 'bout Ronny. Funny how things went 'round in circles, I thought.

"Me an' Jimmy's always been real close, Ronny. He's always sorta looked out for me, ya know? All he knows 'bout you is that you was a part a' that smashed window thing. He's still jus' trying to look out for me."

"You think you need to be protected from me?" he asked, starin' into my eyes.

"What do you think?" I said, noddin' down at his tooth marked hand.

We both smiled.

We hung out together for most a' the rest a' that day. We'd fooled 'round most a' the time—chasin' each other 'round the school buildin' an' climbin' on the jungle bars. We talked a lot, too. Mostly 'bout nothin'. But, every now an' then our conversation would get serious an' I would find out some new little thing 'bout Ronny. I treasured these little bits a' information. I stored them up in my brain so I could think on 'em later, later when we had to part. He told me he'd never met his daddy, that his mother couldn't even be sure who he was. Actually, the way Ronny talked 'bout his mother shocked me—called her a whore the first time he'd mentioned her. I told him not to talk that way 'bout his own mama. He'd gone silent for a while, then said that he was used to sayin' things the way he saw them, but, if I didn't like it, he wouldn't call his mother no whore, 'least not when I was 'round, anyway.

He told me 'bout his sisters. They was six an' three, an' they both looked up to him like some sorta hero. He reckoned the youngest one was real cute. She did crazy things that always made Ronny laugh, like pokin' her tongue at everyone an' spitting in people's faces. He told me 'bout his Black power meetings, too. How they'd been gettin' more far out each time he went to them. He said they'd been gettin' together a collection a' guns an' storin' them at that farm house we'd been to. An' they was always goin' on 'bout wipin' out the pigs, he said. He told me he was gettin' tired a' the whole lot of 'em. Tired of all the hate that came with bein' part a' that crowd. But, he said, he felt like the others was forcin' him to stay with it, always puttin' him on the spot, makin' him say he'd be a part a' whatever crazy thing they was planning.

We was lyin' on the grass under the old oak tree when Ronny'd told me this. I reached over an' put my arm 'round his shoulder.

"Well, it's different now, Ronny," I said, "You've got me now. Together we can pull away from it."

"Ain't that simple, Angel. They don't like it if ya quit. I mean they can get ugly, girl," he said, lookin' down at the ground.

"Ronny, I know ugly." I reminded him 'bout the beatin' I had at the hands a' that White crowd. "Got through that an' we can get through this, too."

"Yeah, I guess we can, Angel," he said.

An' then he kissed me.

†††

It was gettin' on to dark when Ronny an' I finally parted. He'd walked with me back to the start a' my street, where we'd held each other close, tryin' to find some privacy behind that big ol' tree on the corner. I grabbed hold a' his t-shirt as we hugged, not wantin' to let him get away. We'd arranged to meet again tomorrow an' I made him promise to take me to meet his mama an' his sisters, even though he'd snarled somethin' 'bout it bein' a waste a' time.

After 'bout ten minutes he pulled away, sayin' if he didn't free himself to go now, we'd still be there at midnight, caught up in each other's arms. I said I didn't mind that one bit an' he'd said, '"Me too, but I reckon your folks might see it different."

Then he pecked me on the lips an' ran off. My eyes trailed after him, still focusin' on the corner he'd disappeared 'round long after he'd gone. For the first time in a long while, I realized, I was really happy.

When I drifted in through our doorway, no one seemed much interested in what I been up to. Actually, I noticed, this last few months, Mama an' Daddy was lettin' me do my own thing more an' more, without havin' to tell 'em where I'll be every minute a' the day. I was glad to have this sorta independence, but tonight, I thought, it'd be nice to have someone to tell my day to, to share my excitement over Ronny with. I looked at Mama, spoonin' mash onto three plates. All I got from her was a lecture 'bout how I'd have two broke arms if I hadn't been home by the time they was ready to sit down at the dinner table. As it was, she hadn't fixed me anythin', an' it served me right to have a hungry belly tonight.

So, I put a piece a' bread on my plate an', after some more moanin', Mama'd spooned a bit a' mash onto it offa hers. I didn't care that the others had peas an' sausages in front a' them. Spendin' that extra time with Ronny was worth payin' that price.

Daddy an' Jimmy weren't in no mood to hear 'bout my love life.

"All hell's breaking loose down there!" Daddy'd grumbled, nodding down at the front page a' the Birmin'ham Leader that sat on the dinner table beside his plate.

Lookin' across, I read the headline:

COMMITTEE MEMBER ATTACKED

Daddy went on to tell us the decision that'd been made yestaday wasn't too popular with the White folks 'bout town. Those White committee fellas had been called traitors an' the shopkeepers'd sworn that they'd never take down the COLORED signs in their stores, an' no one was gonna make 'em. A'course, ol' Bull Conner'd come out fighting, too—callin' those committee men a bunch a' nigger lovin' pussies an' sayin' he'd be in hell before he gave in to those outside agitators. So, the White folks'd begun marchin' in the streets themselves, Daddy'd said. But it weren't nothin' like our marches. These ones was bein' arranged by men who wore white robes an' hoods—men who called themselves the Ku Klux Klan.

†††

Ronny an' me was walkin' along Maple Avenue. It was gettin' on to dark again, an' I knew soon we'd be apart. I thought 'bout what'd be like if we never had to part, if we could stay together all day—an' all night, too. I smiled at the thought a' us cuddled up in bed, doin' the things that married folks do when they're cuddled up in bed together.

"What you thinkin' 'bout?" Ronny asked.

"Nothin'," I blushed.

"Well, that nothin's sure makin' you go red, girl," he teased me. "Anyway, what'd you think 'bout the ol' lady?"

We'd jus' come from Ronny's place. His mother'd been asleep on the couch when we got there. Sleeping off another hangover, Ronny'd muttered as we went into the backyard to see his sisters. Soon as they saw me, they began teasin' Ronny 'bout havin' a girlfriend, an' when the little one—Talia—started pokin' her tongue at me, the other one—Sheree—told her not to, said that I was gonna be her sister, an' it wasn't polite to poke yer tongue at family. Ronny'd kicked her then an' she'd started cryin' an' ran into the house. Next thing, it was his mother's voice I heard.

"Ronny, can't you shut those damn kids up?" she'd yelled.

"Do it yourself," Ronny shot back. "You're the mother!"

"Ronny!" I said, half under my breath. I was feelin' uneasy, not keen to get caught in the middle of a fight 'tween the two a' them.

He gave me a sorta embarrassed look, an' I could see he wished we wasn't there. Next thing, his mother was leanin' in the doorway. Her hair was all messed up, an' she was squintin' from the sun, but I could tell she was still a fine lookin' woman. She had on a T-shirt that stretched over her full breasts but only came half way down her stomach. Her cutoff jeans showed off her honey brown legs. She only looked in her early twenties, but I figured she must be older than that to have a child Ronny's age.

"What you been up to Ronny?" She smirked at her son, her eyes fixed on me.

"This is Angel," Ronny didn't look at her.

"Hi, Angel," she smiled at me. "My boy been treating you like an angel?"

"Yeah, I guess so," I stammered, feelin' uncomfortable.

'I'll bet he has," she said knowingly. Then she added, "Don't treat her too good, Ronny. Don't need any more snot nosed little mistakes running 'round here now, do we?"

With that, she went back inside.

I looked across at Ronny. In jus' a few seconds, his mother had humiliated him, an' the embarrassment was all over his face.

"Told you she was a whore!" he spat out.

So, when Ronny'd asked me what I thought a' her as we walked down Maple Avenue, I didn't really know what to say.

"I can't tell after only seeing her for half a minute."

"Don't matter if you know her for half a minute or half a lifetime, Angel, she's still—"

"Don't say it, Ronny," I cut him off.

We'd walked on in silence for a few minutes, then he'd begun sayin' 'bout what it'd be like when he had a family. A'course he spoke like it was jus' natural that I was gonna be a part of it.

"We'll have four kids, two boys an' two girls—that way they'll each have someone to play with. An' I'll be their playmate, too, Angel. Not like how most kids are, afraid a' their ol' man. That ain't gonna be the way in our family."

I could see this was makin' Ronny happy, so I let him keep buildin' up this picture a' what it was gonna be like for us a few years down the road. Pretty soon, I was caught up in it too.

"I've always wanted a house with a pond for the birds an' ducks to play in," I said.

"We'll have it all, Angel," he said grandly, "an' our kids won't never even get a notion to call you nothin' but Mama."

As he said that I could see the sadness in his eyes, an' I knew then that he really did care for his mother—he jus' couldn't handle what she said an' done. I was thinkin' of what to say to help him over this, when a loud blast jolted us back to reality. We both swung 'round. There, comin' up the street was that old black beast of a car that I'd come to hate. The car that I'd heard at Fred's meetin' that time. The car that I sat in on the way to that dreadful other meetin'. The car that stood for everythin' I was trying to get Ronny away from.

"Damn!" I whispered.

Ronny squeezed my hand. It was those same two guys as last time sittin' in front. As they got closer, the guy in the passenger seat leaned out an' yelled, "We caught the love birds!" The other guy let out a loud yell an' then they both repeated it together, "We caught the lovebirds!"

"Ronny, they've been drinkin'!" I whispered.

"It's all right, Angel," he tried to comfort me.

The car pulled up alongside us, an' they both spilled out, stumblin' onto the pavement.

"Hoping we'd come across you, Ronny boy," the one who'd been drivin' mumbled. His breath was all over us, that sick smell a' hard liquor.

"Ain't got time for no mushy stuff, now boy," he babbled. "We got bidness to do."

"What's up?" Ronny asked.

"Serious, Ronny," the other one spoke now. "Klan's been doin' some serious crap, man. Bombed King's house, bombed the Gaston. We gotta do somethin' 'bout those fascist pigs, boy!"

I looked at Ronny. *Now's the time Ronny,* I thought. *Now's the time to prove this to me. All the talk in the world don't mean nothin' if you don't stand up now.*

"What ya gonna do?" Ronny asked.

No, Ronny, I thought. *Don't even go there.*

"Jus' gonna go cruising, Ronny," the driver slurred. "But, boy, who knows what we gonna find?"

He winked at me then, an' I gave him a look that made it clear I wasn't gonna play along.

"Now, you gonna drop off your woman first or she comin' too?" He smirked back at me.

"Ronny!" I whispered, grabbin' his arm.

"You guys are drunk," Ronny said, pulling away from me. "You'll drive us to our death 'fore we even see the Klan."

"Drunk!" the driver roared. "Boy, I ain't never been more sober. Now if you's too chicken to mix it with the big boys, don't come up with no wimpy excuses 'bout us bein' drunk!"

"I ain't chicken," Ronny shot back.

Oh, Ronny, I thought, *you've played right into this fool's hand.* I had to jump in.

"But he ain't stupid, neither," I said.

The driver turned to me, an amazed look on his face.

"What the hell is this, Ronny?" he yelled. "Your tart standing up for ya. Where's your pride, boy?"

I waited for Ronny to let him have it then—to put that drunk fool in his place for callin' me a tart. But he never did. Instead, he shot an annoyed look at me.

"Shut up, Angel!" he said.

I felt foolish then. Ronny'd let me down—left me stranded. All the nice words—the dreamin' while we was alone, the promises—all that'd jus' disappeared. But it was worse than that. They was gonna do somethin' crazy tonight an' I knew now that Ronny was goin' with them. Without me, he'd be led into whatever stupid thing they did. I knew I had to save him. The three of 'em was piling into the car.

"You can walk home from here," Ronny nodded at me as the three of 'em piled into the car. His words was harsh soundin', nothin' like the sweet, comfortin' way he'd been speakin' jus' a few minutes ago, before these two'd turned up.

"No," I glared at him. "I'm comin' with you."

The driver let out a hoot an' cried out, "Got you a feisty one there, boy!"

As I climbed into the back a' that horrible black car I jus' knew somethin' terrible was gonna happen.

†††

That ugly smell a' drunkenness was even worse now that we was all shut up in that vehicle together. Those two fools up front was goin' on 'bout what'd happened las' night an' how it was time for some rightin' a' wrongs to be done. Me an' Ronny sat in the back in silence. I tried to make sense outta what they was sayin'—tried to get a picture a' jus' what'd been goin' on. I didn't dare ask any questions. I didn't want to get that driver riled up. I could tell he was the violent one.

Doctor King's hous'd been bombed, the whole place smashed to bits an' him an' his family only jus' scrapin' away with their lives. An' some motel owned by a Black man'd been bombed, too. The room that Doctor King an' the others'd been usin' to hold their meetings'd been totally destroyed. Since then, accordin' to these two, Black folks'd been riotin' in the streets. An' it looked to me, as we rolled our way towards Birmin'ham, like we was on our way to join 'em.

"Where the hell you been hiding anyway, Ronny?" the driver demanded, lookin' at us through the rear vision mirror.

Ronny fidgeted, then mumbled, "Oh, I been sorta busy."

"Hey, boy," the driver's voice was sharper now. "You ain't never too busy for the movement." Then he turned to the other guy. "I reckon ol' Ronny's gettin' soft, man. Reckon he's too busy chasing his piece a' tail to have time for us."

The other guy nodded. "Yeah, man. I always knew he never had the balls for it."

I knew they was jus' tryin' to bait Ronny, to lead him on so he'd agree to whatever dare they came out with next. I looked across at Ronny. His teeth was clenched an' his eyes stared at the back a' the seat in front a' him. I knew he was gettin' worked up.

"Told ya before," he finally blurted out, "I ain't chicken!"

"Good!" the driver shot back. "Then you can look after the shooter."

He swerved the car onto the gravel roadside an' skidded to a standstill. Then he reached across an' opened the glove box. He pulled out a gun. It was the first real gun I ever seen. It was black, jus' like the car, an' smaller than I imagined a real gun would be. But it still had a trigger an' a barrel, an' I knew that those two bits was enough to kill someone. I suddenly felt scared. As the driver passed the gun to Ronny, I found myself reaching across to grab Ronny's hand—to stop him from taking hold a' that thing.

"No, Ronny," I blurted out. "Don't take it!"

The driver pulled back then. He twisted the gun up so that he was holding it by the handle, an' pointed it at me.

"Bang!" he said. Then him an' the other guy started laughin'.

Suddenly that driver was serious again.

"Take the damn gun, Ronny!" he yelled.

This time he threw it back to Ronny, who caught it in his lap. I watched Ronny pick that gun up an' run it through his hands, rubbin' his palms over the barrel. Only hours ago he'd been rubbin' those same hands through my hair, talkin' to me 'bout love. Now, here he was, makin' love to this symbol a' hate. I turned away, lookin' out the window, an' my eyes began waterin' over.

†††

It was gettin' on to dark when we hit the outskirts a' town. But instead a' the riotin' that was supposed to be goin' on, things 'round there seemed real quiet. As we cruised 'round the factories an' car wreck yards, those two up front kept their eyes peeled for any sign a' life, anythin' that could lead to some action. They was still talkin' big—steppin' Ronny out 'bout not knowin' how to use that gun now. I jus' sat there, bit my lip, an' wished I was someplace else.

"Over there!" the guy in the passenger seat said, pointin' towards a scrap yard.

We all looked. A White kid on a bike had jus' come 'round the corner. He jumped off his bike an' started climbin' the wire mesh fence a' that yard.

"Hot dang!" the driver laughed. "The little prick's tryin' to break into that damn wrecker's yard."

We watched that kid struggle to climb over the fence. There was barbed wire on the top an' he was real careful not to get caught. Even still, his jeans got stuck on the way over an' he fell to the other side, with a rip down one leg. He jumped up an' started rummagin' through the piles a' junk, lookin' for who knows what.

"Got him cornered," the driver sneered, as we cruised towards the wreckin' yard. That White kid had his back towards us, so we was able to get right up alongside that fence before he noticed us. It was only when the driver revved the engine that he spun 'round.

He was terrified. He backed up against that pile a' junk an' froze. As he stood there I could see that his eyes was busy, searchin' out a place to run. But, he soon discovered, there was nowhere. He was trapped. So, he jus' stood there tremblin', waitin' for someone to get outta that car. The front door opened an' out came the driver. The kid gasped when he realized it was a Black man who was facin' him.

"What ya doin' here, boy?" the driver demanded.

From where I sat, I could hear the fear in that kid's reply.

"Just, just ... looking for a ball I lost."

"Jus' lookin' for a ball I lost," the driver repeated, mockin' him. "What you think I am, boy?" His voice was scary now. "Some dumb ignorant nigger? Huh?"

The kid's eyes was wide open, his face white as a ghost.

"No suh," he whimpered.

"Then don't crap me, boy," he stepped up to the fence, takin' hold a' the wire meshin'.

"You're a damn thief an' I've caught ya red-handed, haven't I boy?"

I noticed the kid's jeans go wet an' a puddle formin' at his shoe. He'd wet himself.

"Yes suh," he finally said.

"Well, I'm makin' a citizen's arrest on you, boy. Now, you got ten seconds to get your ass back over here 'fore I come over an' get ya."

The kid was shakin' as he moved up to the fence. When he put a foot into the mesh to begin climbin', it slipped. He tried again, an' slipped again.

"Don't you be crappin' me, boy!"

"No suh."

He was cryin' now. Still, this time he managed to get his footin'. His arms was shakin' as he pulled himself up. He made slow progress up that fence, but when he got to the top, he didn't even care 'bout gettin' caught on the barb wire. I guess, he knew that gettin' a scratch from the wire was the least a' his problems now. Once over the top, he seemed to let go an' fell down in a heap at the feet a' the driver. The driver's boot plowed into his stomach.

"That's for lying to me, White boy," he said.

The kid started coughin'. The driver pulled him to his feet an' pushed him towards the car.

"Get in back, boy," he ordered.

The kid fumbled to open the door. Ronny slid towards me.

"Ronny, don't be a part a' this," I whispered, grabbin' his arm.

That White kid was in the car with us now. He looked maybe sixteen or seventeen, but he was sobbin' like a little kid. He cowered in the corner, his eyes dancin' round the car, first to the driver, then Ronny, the passenger an' finally, he looked at me. His eyes seemed to be reachin' out to me, pleadin' for help, beggin' me. Maybe he thought that, 'cause I was a girl, I would be the easiest on him.

I felt so sorry for this kid, but what could I do? I felt jus' as trapped as he was. I looked down at the gun cradled in Ronny's lap. The White kid followed my eyes, an' when he saw it, he let out a yell. Ronny looked across at him an', realizin' what'd caused him to panic, he stuffed the gun under his shirt. The White kid looked up into Ronny's face, as if to ask if Ronny meant to hurt him. I looked at Ronny, too. His face was full a' confusion. He was jus' as trapped as me an' that White kid. I knew what was goin' on in Ronny's head—a battle between what he knew was right an' what was easy. A'course, the easy thing was to go along with the two up front, to terrorize this White kid, to be a man. The hard thing was to stand up for what he believed in, to stand up for us. I made up my mind then that if Ronny couldn't do that, I had to do it—for both of us!

We was cruisin' back outta town now. The driver kept lookin' through the rear vision mirror at that poor White kid. Him an' the other guy was tauntin' him, callin' him a honky an' askin' him if he'd said his prayers this mornin'.

"Hey, girl," the driver's eyes was on me. "What's your name, again?"

"Angel," I said, without enthusiasm.

He snickered to himself.

"Yeah, that's what I thought. Well, you should know better 'an any of us, you bein' an angel, an' all. You reckon the God that honky piece a' crap there prays to is White or Black?"

He snickered again, proud a' himself for bein' so clever. The other guy joined in.

"Dunno," I said, between clenched teeth. The more this guy carried on the more I was beginnin' to hate him.

"Oh, come on girl," he sneered at me. "What 'bout the angels. What color they be?'

The other guy jumped in to answer.

"Only pictures I seen they been White," he said.

"'Course they be White," the driver echoed him, "an' any fool knows that the creator's a nigger. Damn Bible tells us that."

Now he was focusin' on the White kid again.

"You listenin' to me, honky boy?"

The kid looked up, an' through his snifflin' managed to say, "Yessuh."

"Well, you better be. Because this is real important stuff, boy. They don't teach you this down at your lily White Klan schools, now."

He carried on drivin' for 'bout a minute before he spoke again. I hoped he'd jus' shut up an' give us all a rest until we got to wherever we was headin'. But then he started up again.

"What color them angels, boy?"

The White kid was lookin' out the window an' didn't even realize he was bein' spoken to.

"Ronny!" the driver screamed.

"Yeah?" Ronny's voice was unsteady.

"That honky thinks he's too good for us niggers. Too high an' mighty to answer our questions. Where's that piece a' yours, boy?"

Ronny looked embarrassed as he pulled the gun out from under his shirt. The White kid trembled.

"See that there piece, honky?" the driver was yellin' at the White kid now.

"Yessuh," the kid said.

"Well, that chamber's got six rounds an' only three of 'em's loaded. Now, I'm gonna ask you some questions, an' if you get one wrong, Ronny here gonna shoot a round into your foot. Got it?"

The kid's whole body went tense. Still he managed to mutter a nervous, "Yessuh."

"What color them angels, boy?"

"White, suh."

"An' what color God almighty be?"

"Black suh?"

"'Course he's Black, you fool. Now, boy what you reckon that nigger God do if those lily white angels started gettin' uppity 'bout havin' to minister to a darky? What he do if they said we ain't gonna do your biddin' no more, Mister Nigger God. Go find yuhself some nigger angels to do it instead. What he do, boy?"

The White kid was bitin' his lip. He must've been wonderin' what it was that the driver wanted to hear.

"What he do, boy?"

'Umm ... I reckon he'd destroy them, suh."

The driver smiled.

"Damn right he would, boy. You doin' well, son. Jus' got one more question for ya. If God almighty, the highest, most intelligent person in the whole damn universe, if he'd kill those racist White sons a' bitches, then why should I spare you?"

"I—uh—I dunno, suh."

†††

We'd stopped in a clearin' a few miles from where we picked the White kid up. We'd driven offa the road an' into the bushes for 'bout ten minutes to get to this spot. The two up front seemed pretty confident that we wouldn't be disturbed out here. They hauled the kid outta the back seat an' tossed him into the clearin'. Ronny an' me climbed outta the car.

"What you gonna do?" I demanded a' the driver.

He looked at me the same way he did when I told him Ronny wasn't stupid an' grinned.

"Why, we's gonna have us a trial, Miss Angel," he declared sarcastically. "That's what we gonna do."

"What sorta trial?" Ronny asked. I watched the other guy as he pulled a rope outta the trunk a' the car.

"We's gonna put this here fine piece a' White southern manhood on trial, Ronny boy," the driver snarled as he looked down at the White kid, bunched up on the ground. "Now let's get these here proceedin's underway."

The other guy was wrappin' that rope 'round the kid's hands an' feet, forcin' it so tight that I could see it cuttin' into his wrists.

"We ain't gonna let you hurt him!" I said with a voice that surprised me.

The guy with the rope stopped his work an' looked up at me in amazement. The driver seemed to not even hear what I said. He moved past us, headin' back towards the car to get somethin'. But, as he passed by Ronny an' me, he suddenly stopped an' swung his shoulder towards me. I caught his open fist full on my mouth an' the force of it sent me flyin' to the ground. As the tears welled up in my eyes, I could feel myself swallowing my own blood.

"Wanna learn her to shut the—"

He didn't get any further. From where I lay on the ground, I could see Ronny with his arm outstretched an' that gun pokin' into the driver's face.

"Shut up, man!" Ronny growled.

"Ronny," the driver took a step back, "a man can't put up with bein' ordered 'round by a tart. Come on, man!"

Ronny saw red then. He closed the gap between the two of 'em an' brought the gun back, to send it crushin' down into the driver's cheek.

"Don't call her that," he screamed as blood oozed from the gash that'd opened up on the driver's left cheekbone.

"You ain't no man!" Ronny spat out. "A man don't knock 'round a girl who's already got a broke arm."

He paused. I looked to see what the other guy was doin'. He was still on the ground with the White kid's feet in his hands. He didn't dare move.

"'An' you know how she got that broke arm?" Ronny continued.

For once, the driver was silent.

"She got it marchin' in the damn street for you!"

I saw Ronny lurch forward an' then I heard a click. He'd pulled the trigger. There was no bullet. I jumped up an' ran towards Ronny.

"Ronny," I yelled. "Don't shoot him!"

"Get back, Angel," he commanded, glancing in my direction.

In that instant the driver made his move. He grabbed at the gun with one hand an' sent the other flying towards Ronny's head. But Ronny was too quick. He pulled back so that both hands missed their targets. Now he was holdin' that gun in both a' his hands, his arms outstretched.

"Think you're so damn tough," he blurted into the driver's face. "Kidnap a White kid, huh! Man you make me sick!"

Ronny was so angry that I could see his arms tremblin'. Sweat was running down the driver's face.

"Come on, Ronny," he pleaded. "Listen, man, I'm real sorry for haulin' out your woman but don't go turnin' your back on the brothers."

"The brothers!" Ronny threw the words back at him. "Man, you ever heard of a brother called Josiah Reeby?" He was screaming now.

The driver didn't answer.

"Josiah Reeby was a brother jus' like this brother." Ronny motioned to the White kid on the ground. "He was goin' along, minding his own bidness when a bunch a' cowards kidnapped him an' murdered him."

"So, ain't someone gotta pay for that, Ronny?" The driver looked confused.

"Oh, sure," Ronny's voice was calmer now. "Eye for an eye, right. Well, eye for an eye only gonna make the whole world blind, man." He began shaking his head. "I ain't gonna be part a' your crap no more." Ronny nodded towards the other guy. "Now, I want you two to get in that damn car an' get the hell outta here. Jus' leave us alone. Got it?"

"Yeah, Ronny," the driver said, "we're gone, man."

Ronny kept the gun trained on the driver's head as the two of 'em piled back into the car. From the safety a' the front seat, they managed to get a bit a' courage back, the driver mumblin' 'bout how Ronny's turned into a pussy an' the other guy sayin' over an' over, "Bad crap, man." Then they was gone.

I looked at Ronny, the gun hangin' loose at his side now. I felt so proud a' what he'd done, even if it had taken a gun to give him the courage to do it. Ronny looked at me for the first time since we'd got outta that car. He reached out to me, wipin' away the blood that I could feel tricklin' down my chin.

"I'm sorry, Angel," he mumbled.

"What for?" I looked into his eyes.

"For bein' a coward." He wouldn't meet my stare.

I grabbed hold a' his hand.

"Ronny, listen to me," I said. "That whole thing was a test. An' the thing is you came through it. You didn't give in to those drunk fools."

"Yeah," he sighed, "got myself some guts with a gun in my hand."

"So?" I pressed myself into him. "So, you ain't perfect. But I don't want perfect. I want you."

He put both arms 'round me an' pulled me close. I watched the gun drop to the ground.

†††

That White kid was still on the ground, the rope still cuttin' into his skin. I noticed for the first time that his t-shirt was soaked with sweat. He'd calmed down some now. He must've realized that the danger'd left when that black car'd taken off. Ronny went to him an' began undoin' the rope 'round his wrists. I sat on the ground beside them.

"What's your name," I asked him, massagin' my chin with my free hand.

He looked at me an' smiled.

"Trevor," he said. "Trevor Lemars."

He was lookin' at me strangely now.

"I know you," he said. "You're that girl who got her picture put in the paper."

"You mean that girl that you people nearly killed?" Ronny added harshly.

"Jus' like our people nearly killed him, Ronny," I said.

Ronny freed Trevor's hands now. As he started workin' on his feet he said, "What you people got against us anyway?"

Trevor looked at him.

"I got nothing against you, man."

This was the first time me, an' I suppose Ronny too, had got to talk to a White kid like this. Any other conversation'd been like a master an' slave but all a' those barriers'd been torn apart by what'd happened over the last half hour. Now we was jus' three kids tryin' to make sense out of a crazy world.

"But White people," Ronny said. "Why they hate us so much?"

Trevor looked jus' as confused 'bout that as Ronny was.

"I guess it's because they're afraid of you," he said.

"Why they afraid of us?" I asked.

"Because they don't know you?" he said.

"Don't wanna know us, either," Ronny added.

I remembered somethin' Miss Hattie'd said once.

"I guess it's fear a' the unknown," I said. "Fear a' change."

"Yeah, thats it," Trevor picked up on my words. "They're afraid of change."

I could see that this was somethin' new for Trevor, too, this talkin' with us like we were. I wondered if he'd ever even talked to Black folks before.

"Were you taught to hate Black people?" I wanted to make the most a' this—to try to step into a White person's shoes. Maybe, jus' maybe, then I could start to understan' 'em.

"Well, yeah, I guess so," he said, massagin' his wrists. "My old man's a racist. Remember when I was only 'bout three an' saw my first...colored person." He paused before saying that word—colored—not sure if it was the right one to use in front of us. "I looked at the man an' said to my dad, 'Look, dad, a man covered in chocolate.' You know what he said to me?"

"What?"

"He said, 'No, son, that's a nigger.'"

Ronny finished undoin' Trevor's ropes an' he was sittin' beside me now. "So, your ol' man in the Klan?" he asked.

I could feel that Ronny was kinda uncomfortable with this, that he couldn't totally let go a' the bitterness he'd always known towards White folks. So, his words had a sharp edge to 'em.

"No, 'least I don't think so," Trevor said thoughtfully. "He's jus' your average, run of the mill Alabama racist. He wouldn't see you as a person, as someone who'd jus' saved his boy's life. All he'd see is a word—Black."

"So, he's ignorant," I cut in.

"I guess so." Trevor didn't seem troubled to be talkin' this way 'bout his father. "He's jus' following on with what he's been brought up to know."

"So, what makes you any different?" Ronny's words was harsh.

"Well, I don't know."

As I listened to Trevor, I thought back to the other day when me an' Ronny'd really spoken for the first time in my livin' room. This was what this was like—cuttin' through all the wasted words to get to what our hearts was feelin'. I wondered why people couldn't always talk like this, why there was so much pretendin' that always went on, so many wasted words.

"Few years back," Trevor continued, "we learned 'bout the war in Germany an' what Hitler did to the Jews. I saw my teacher standing up there—a teacher who everybody knew hated colored people—telling us how bad Hitler was, an' I thought to myself 'you hypocrite'. Since then I've tried to see people as people." He looked at me now. "Then, when I saw what was happening in the streets over the last couple weeks, an', when I saw that picture of you in the paper, I actually felt ashamed of what was happening to y'all."

He was focusin' on my arm, still in its sling.

"Damned ashamed," he repeated.

"You ever read the Bible?" I asked him.

"Sure. Reckon I'm a Christian—best I can be, anyways."

"You know what it says at John chapter sixteen, verse thirty-three?"

I was thinkin' a' Josiah.

"Not off the top of my head?" he said.

I quoted it for him then, word for word. I told him 'bout Josiah, 'bout how they found him with that scripture in his pocket. He said he'd heard 'bout how some Black kid'd been hung, how it'd made him feel sick. Throughout all a' this Ronny'd sat in silence, starin' at the ground in front a' him.

"I reckon we can all conquer, like Jesus did," I said.

"How we do that?" Trevor asked.

"By not followin' the pattern that they've set for us," I said, noddin' at him an' Ronny. 'By sitting here, like we are, not two Black an' one White, but jus' three human beings, by jus' doin' that we're conquerin'."

He looked at me an' smiled.

"Yeah, I think you're right," he said.

We talked on for some time in that clearin' in the bushes. It was almos' as if we didn't want to stop talkin' an' go our separate ways, didn't want to have to fit back into our roles a' White an' Black. After a while, though, we started thinkin' 'bout our situation. It must've been close on to ten o'clock by now an' we was stranded in the forest, far from home. An' not only that, but we was on the outskirts a' Birmin'ham—an' the Klan was in an ugly mood.

Trevor was worried 'bout us. He said there was plenty a' rednecks who'd be cruisin' 'round lookin' for trouble. He wanted to stay with us, but Ronny said if he got caught with us, he'd be strung up first for bein' a nigger lover. So, we walked out to the main road together, an' then parted company—him goin' north back to Birmin'ham an' us south to Harpersville. I hugged Trevor before we'd parted an' he'd whispered in my ear that someday Birmin'ham would realize who it's real heroes were. As Ronny an' me walked away, I asked who he thought Trevor meant by that.

"I reckon he was talkin' 'bout you, Angel," Ronny said.

†††

The darkness a' the night made that long walk home seem

even more terrifyin'. Every step in that blackness was an ordeal, a risk I wished I didn't have to be takin'. With everythin' that'd already gone on tonight, I was already feelin' exhausted—my emotions all used up. Yet, here we were, all alone in the night an' facing all the dangers our minds could dream up. Ronny an' I held hands as we walked along in silence. The sweat made our palms all wet an' clammy. That sweat, streamin' down from our armpits, across our forearms an' into our joined palms, told each of us jus' how scared the other one was.

I tried to think 'bout other things, to keep my min' busy so it wouldn't haunt me. But, no matter how much I tried to concentrate on Miss Hattie, on the future life that me an' Ronny'd dreamed up earlier or even on that first meetin' when I heard Doctor King speak, no matter how hard I tried to think on these things, my mind jus' couldn't escape the image a' poor Josiah Reeby bein' dragged away into a pitch black night, an' the expectation that I was gonna be next. Ronny finally spoke. His voice was slow an' deliberate.

"I'm gonna have to get outta town for a while."

I looked across, jus' able to make out his face in the blackness. His words had taken me by surprise.

"What you talking 'bout Ronny?"

"They're gonna be after me," he spoke coldly. "Ain't gonna let this slide."

I knew he was right. That driver was crazy enough an' stupid enough to go after Ronny for what'd happened.

"But, Ronny," I said, squeezin' his hand, "you're gonna have to face them some time. If you start runnin' now, you'll always be runnin'."

"No, Angel," he said. "It'll blow over. Soon as he gets over his hurt pride. Might take a week, might take a few months. But, until then, there ain't no telling what he'll do."

"I'll go with you," I blurted out.

"You can't, Angel," he sighed. "We ain't ready for that yet. In a few years, but not yet."

I knew he was right.

"I don't want you to go," I pleaded.

"Only be for a short while," he said. "Then I'll be back."

Before I could reply, the noise of a car's engine filled the air. We could see headlights beamin' towards us off in the distance. A shiver a' fear ran through me. We'd been walkin' in the middle a' the road, but now Ronny pushed me over to the side an' told me to lie down in the grass an' wait for that car to go by. I held my breath as that car got closer. As those headlights got bigger, I noticed another light, dancin' 'round in the bushes an' long grass. Whoever was in that car had a flashlight.

"Ronny!" I whispered.

"I'm here," he put his arm over my shoulder. "Keep down!"

The car was nearly upon us now, the whir a' the engine deafenin' in that still night. As I shivered in the long grass, I recognized somethin' in that sound. That engine. It sounded familiar. I thought 'bout it for a second, then realized that it sounded jus' like the noise that Jimmy's engine made. The beam from that flashlight was above us, an' then an unmistakable voice rose above the whir a' that motor, a voice that brought tears a' relief to my eyes.

"Angel!"

It was Jimmy. I jumped up an' started towards my brother's voice. The flashlight shone in my face.

"Angel!" Jimmy's voice rang out a second time.

The car shuddered to a stop, an' then Jimmy was runnin' 'cross the road towards me. I looked for Ronny. He was still lyin' in the grass, same as we was when we thought this was a White person's car. I grabbed for his hand. He pulled away.

"Go on, Angel," he whispered. "Go to your brother. Leave

me here."

"No, Ronny," I said. "It'll be all right."

"Angel," Jimmy called out. "Who's there with you?"

Ronny stood up then. Jimmy was upon us now. He hugged me close to him an' then shone his flashlight on the other figure beside me. He glared across at Ronny, keeping that flashlight trained on his face.

"What the hell you been up to?"

I didn't know if Jimmy was talkin' to me or Ronny. I broke free from my brother's arms.

"Jimmy," I said, placing myself between the two of 'em. "Me an' Ronny was kidnapped. We was dumped a few miles up the road." I had to lie. I knew if I told Jimmy 'bout those other two guys, he'd only blame Ronny for gettin' me mixed up with 'em in the first place. "We thought you was them comin' back for us," I added.

"Kidnapped?" Jimmy glared at me. "Kidnapped from where?"

"From Marple Avenue, jus' 'round from Ronny's place," I replied.

That reminded Jimmy that Ronny was there, an' he fixed his eyes back on him.

"I told you that nothing but trouble'd come from hangin' out with him," he scoffed. "Now, get in the damn car."

He turned to go. I looked back at Ronny who hadn't moved an inch since he'd sprung to his feet.

"Jimmy," I said, "what 'bout Ronny?'

"He can walk," Jimmy snapped.

"Then I'm walking, too," I yelled.

I couldn't believe Jimmy could be so childish 'bout this. He spun 'round.

"Daddy sent me out to bring you home, Angel, an' that's what I'm gonna do."

He grabbed my good arm.

"Girl, you're gettin' in that car, even if I have to drag you into it."

"Not without Ronny!" I insisted.

Jimmy flashed his light back into Ronny's face then.

"I don't like you, Jackson," he said.

I closed my eyes as Jimmy spoke. It was the voice a' one a' those White racists I was hearing, comin' outta by brother's throat.

"You're a little troublemaker, an' I ain't happy 'bout you mixin' with my sister. Now, if you ever bring harm to her, you're in big trouble, you hear me?"

Ronny was forced to shade his eyes from that light. He looked straight back at Jimmy.

"Yeah, I hear ya," he said.

"All right, get in the damn car," Jimmy took the light off Ronny. "Both a' ya."

I ran across to Ronny an' let him put his arm 'round my shoulder. We made our way over to the car an' both climbed in back. As Jimmy climbed into the driver's seat he mumbled on 'bout how worried Mama an' Daddy was 'bout me an' how he'd had to give up his Sunday evenin' riskin' his neck jus' to find us makin' out in a paddock an' didn't I think this was stretchin' brotherly love jus' a little too far? Me an' Ronny let him go on, happy to jus' sink into each other's arms an' stare out into the night.

ChapterEIGHT
ALABAMA, LATE MAY 1963

Two weeks passed by since that crazy night. Ronny'd gone, jus' like he said he would. Turned out that Jim Bevel was organisin' a group to be a part a' what was called a Freedom Ride—somethin' 'bout travellin' between the states on a Greyhoun' bus. Seemed to us like jus' the thing for Ronny to get away for a while. So, he'd approached Jim himself an' sorta auditioned for a spot on that bus. Jim'd been quite suspicious a' him at first, Ronny'd told me. But, after a while, he'd got to see that Ronny was jus' the sorta kid he was lookin' for—serious, determined an' focused.

It tore me apart havin' to watch Ronny slip away from me. But I knew it had to be like this an' so I made myself be strong. I didn't cry in front a' him—even though I was cryin' inside.

Life without Ronny was miserable. It was a struggle jus' to get through each day. I couldn't stop thinkin' 'bout him. I was aching to be with him, wishin' he was here with me. I felt like I would go crazy if I didn't do somethin' to try an' force my mind offa him.

That was the state I was in when Mister Newton pulled me aside after school one Friday. It was the same day I got my arm outta that sling an' I felt relieved to be free of it. I was lookin' forward to running down the street on the way home with both arms swingin' free. I thought a' Ronny then, too, a' bein' able to put both arms 'round him an' pull him close to me.

"I've got a proposal for you, Angel," Mister Newton'd said after the other kids'd filed outta the classroom.

I stood at his desk, a questionin' look on my face.

"What sorta proposal, Mister Newton?" I asked.

He leaned back in his chair.

"I've been very impressed with how you've handled yourself over the last few weeks," he said. "I've seen real leadership qualities coming through in you, Angel."

He pulled a folder outta his desk drawer an' dropped it on the desk. I looked down at the words scrawled across the front of it in thick black crayon:

Freedom Schools.

"Ever fancied yourself as a teacher, Angel?" he asked.

"A teacher?"

"Yes, Angel," he was gettin' that familiar excitement in his voice now. "We're organizing classes for the younger kids—ages six through nine—to teach them some Black heritage. A kind of miniature version of what we've been doing in our lunch breaks. I want you to be one of the instructors."

I didn't say nothin'. Jus' stared down at that folder on his desk. Me, a teacher a' Black heritage? Feedin' hungry little minds? Could I really do that? Could I?

"Angel," he tried to get my attention.

I looked up at him.

"Do you want to do it?"

I didn't even try to hide my enthusiasm.

"Yes," I said. "Oh, yes."

†††

Mama'd relaxed her stand on my seeing Miss Hattie. Told me

I was so headstrong that I was bound to go off an' do somethin' else crazy with or without Miss Hattie's influence. Least if I was 'round there, she figured, she wouldn't have to fret 'bout me cavortin' in no bushes at all hours a' the night. An', anyways, she'd added, maybe that silly ol' woman's fool ideas'll stop me from actin' so boy crazy all a' the time.

So, I headed for Miss Hattie's place after school that day. I had to tell her my news. It felt good to walk up to her balcony again, to take in the smells from her overgrown garden. But, at the same time it felt strange. I almost felt like I was an adult returnin' to a place I last visited as a child. I looked over at the old rockin' chair on Miss Hatties' balcony an' I realized I was no longer that little kid who used to snuggle up in her lap on Sunday aftanoons. So much'd happened to me over the last few weeks. It'd made me older, changed me—made me grow up.

Miss Hattie's front door was closed. That seemed strange, it bein' another one a' those stinkin' hot Alabama summer Fridays. I banged on the door. No answer. I banged again, then yelled out to her. Still nothin'. That's weird, I thought. Miss Hattie's normally home this time a' day. She must'nt've been far away. So, I decided to hang 'round. I sat down in Miss Hattie's rockin' chair an' pulled my homework book an' a pen from outta my schoolbag. I carefully ripped out the middle page an', leanin' it on the front a' the book, I began writin':

Dear Ronny,

I miss you so much. All I wanna do is sleep. More I sleep, quicker the days'll go by an' sooner you'll be coming back to me. Anyway Ronny, I got me some good news today. You'll never believe it but Mister Newton wants me to be a teacher. To teach younger kids about Black stuff. You reckon I can pull that off? Me, I don't know—but I'll give it a go anyway.

I got that far an' paused. This was the third letter I wrote to Ronny since he'd been away. In those last ones I told him 'bout how I missed him so much an' then filled him in on all a' the news 'bout what was happenin' 'round here, an' that was it. But today, I wanted to say more than that. I wanted to tell Ronny Jackson exactly how I felt 'bout him. I knew how I felt but the words jus' wouldn't come. I sat there for 'bout five minutes, my feet restin' on Miss Hattie's balcony, my hand doodlin' in the top corner a' the page, an' my eyes starin' off into space before I got another word down. But once I did, the rest of it jus' flowed out:

I'm really proud of what you been able to do, Ronny Jackson. I know how hard it is to stand up for what you believe in, 'specially when others are pushin' you to go against it. Jimmy called that peer pressure and he said it's the hardest thing anyone can ever face. Well, I reckon you faced it, Ronny. An' even though you're away now and that hurts, I'm proud a' what you're doing for the movement. Real proud Ronny. And Ronny, just wanted to tell you that I love you.

That was the first time I actually ever said those words to anyone, 'cept my family. A'course, I said it in my head a thousand times an', sure, I told Jimmy that time that I loved Ronny. But now I was sayin' it direct to Ronny himself. By writing it down like this, makin' an on paper record a' my feelin's, I was finally acceptin' that this was real, that all the stallin', all the barriers, all the could never bes was gone. I was thirteen years ol' an' I'd foun' the first love a' my life. An' for me, I knew, there'd be no one else—no one like Ronny.

"Angel Dunbar!"

The voice startled me, makin' me scratch a line across the page. I looked across the yard from where it'd come an' saw Miss Hattie swingin' open the gate. I quickly stuffed my homework book with its ripped out middle page back into my bag. I was careful to fold the half-finished letter in two an' drop that in as well. By the time Miss Hattie joined me on the balcony I had hid all evidence of my love letter safely away.

"What you doin' here, girl?" she quizzed me.

"Jus' visitin'," I replied taking my feet offa her balcony. "Where you been, Miss Hattie?"

She walked past me, into the house.

"I been keeping busy," she called back to me.

I followed her inside.

"Nothing for you to worry 'bout," she added.

I made my way to the kitchen table. She'd disappeared into the bathroom.

"Got some good news," I called out to her.

"Good news, Angel?" she called back. "Only news you'd think'd be good is if our Mister Jackson was comin' home."

She was back in the kitchen with me now, her face fresh from a dunkin' a' cold water.

"No, it ain't that good," I replied as she sat at the other side a' the table.

"Then how good is it, girl?"

She fixed her eyes on me for the first time.

"I'm gonna be a teacher, Miss Hattie." I blurted the words out, like an excited kid.

"You're gonna be a teacher." She repeated the words slowly. "What kinda teacher, Angel?"

I couldn't help feelin' that she was only giving me half a' her attention. The way her eyes seemed to be lookin' straight past me told me she had somethin' else on her mind.

I went on to tell her 'bout my little meetin' with Mister Newton—how I would be taking the classes on Sataday afternoons an' how Mister Newton was gonna give me help durin' the week to get the lessons together.

"Sounds like jus' the thing you need," she said absent-mindedly.

I looked across at her. "What you thinkin' bout, Miss Hattie?" I asked.

"Aw nothing," she murmured. "Jus' figurin' on what a fine school teacher you'd make."

I knew she was lyin'. "Come on, Miss Hattie." I leaned across the table. "You don't have to hide things from me."

She looked across at me then. I knew she was fightin' over whether to let me in on this or not. She stood up an' walked to the basin.

"You're right, Angel," she said, lookin' out the window. "I don't have to. But, girl, sometimes people hold things back because they want to. Because they love someone. An' that's what I'm doin' right now." She turned 'n focused her stare on me. "Don't be asking me, Angel, 'cause I won't be saying," she said firmly. Then, as if to wipe those thoughts from both our minds, she added, "So when you gonna begin this school teacherin'?"

For her it might've been easy to switch subjects. But not me. Whatever it was that she was keepin' from me kept naggin' away at me, raisin' all sorts a' questions. We'd chatted on for another twenty minutes or so. After that, I made an excuse to leave.

For the first time I could ever remember I walked away from that ol' woman's house feelin' worse than when I got there.

✝✝✝

"Leave her alone!" I screamed.

I was beginnin' to lose my temper. The twelve kids who was sprawled out before me looked like angels—girls with cute pigtails an' boys with chubby cheeks. But, I was soon discoverin', looks could be deceivin'. I didn't know which was worse, the boys in the back who kept pullin' the girl's hair an' pokin' 'em in the ribs or the girls up front who kept whisperin' to each other an' gigglin'.

It was so hot that I decided we'd have our first Sataday class outside, under the shade a' that ol' oak tree in the corner a' the school grounds. But as the kids played up more an' more, I began thinkin' maybe we'd be better off inside. After all, it was better to lose control of a bunch a' pint sized brats indoors where no one walkin' by could see you an' mutter to themselves that girl ain't cut out for no school teacherin'. But it was too late. We was out here now an' I was gonna have to make the most a' this. I pushed on with the lesson.

"Who knows where we came from?"

The two girls closest to me began whisperin', then gigglin'. One of 'em put up her hand.

"Yes," I nodded to her.

"Well," she snickered, "I came from forty-two Seventh Avenue an' Joyce came from fifty-one Mayberry Avenue."

All the girls started laughin'. The boys jus' looked at them like they was crazy. I waited for the noise to die down.

"I mean Black people," I tried again. "Where did Black people come from?"

A boy at the back called out, "Af'ica."

"That's right," I said, hoping, that I was finally gettin' somewhere.

"Now who knows where Africa is?"

Mister Newton'd given me an old map a' the world, which I spread out before them, placin' a twig on each corner to keep it down.

All the hands went up along with excited cries of "me, me."

I pointed to the boy in the back who'd been pokin' the most ribs. I was tryin' out somethin' that Mister Newton'd told me—

to keep the naughtiest kid busy so he'd be too distracted to play up. He jumped to his feet an' strutted up to the map.

"Show us," I encouraged him.

"Easy," he leaned down to the map.

"Af'ica right here."

He poked a dirty finger at South America. The girl who'd spoken up before—the one who lived on Seventh Avenue—snickered.

"No it ain't," she scoffed.

The kid with the dirty fingers spun 'round an' glared at her.

"Shut ya ugly face!" he spat out.

"Make me, drongo!"

"That's enough," I said forcefully. But I was too late. He'd already lunged at her, smashin' his foot into her side. Now she was cryin'.

"Leave her alone!" I grabbed the boy by the arm an' pulled him away from the girl, who was now threatenin' to tell on him to a real teacher.

Why did I ever agree to this, I wondered as I looked over the group. I stood up an' began raisin' my voice, tellin' them to be quiet an' sit still. I was 'bout to start in on this lecture 'bout how we all knew I weren't no real teacher but that don't mean they can get away with murder when a sharp sound made me look across the field. What I saw there made me flinch. The kids noticed my reaction an' all their heads twisted 'round to see what it was that'd startled me. As I looked towards the parkin' lot, I felt a sinkin' feelin' inside a' me. An urge to run came over me. But I knew I couldn't. These dozen kids was my respons'bility. I had to stay here an' stand my ground.

I watched that horrible black car—that car I hoped to never see again—as it cruised 'round in a slow circle. I could feel a hot flush in my face. But then a voice inside my head was commandin' me:

control yourself, get back on track, ignore it.

I sat down an' gave a sharp clap with my hands.

"This way please," I said shakily.

The kids must've sensed somethin' was up 'cause they all obeyed me.

"Now Africa," I said, leanin' down to the map, desperate to get this lesson back on track, "is over here." I pointed to it. "See how big it is."

The kids was silent. I stole a look at the car. It'd come right up onto the field now an' was slowly bearin' down on us, like a lion closin' in for the kill, I thought.

"But Africa ain't jus' one country." My voice was shaky now. "It's a whole lot of 'em. Africa is what we call a continent."

Rather than distractin' them from the danger, my words— each one more nervous than the last—was causin' the kids to turn an' look at the car.

"Who's that?" the boy with the dirty fingers demanded.

"I don't know," I tried to sound in control. "Now let's get back to Africa shall we?"

"What they want with us?" another kid asked, totally ignorin' what I jus' said.

"Could be the Klan come to ram burnin' crosses down our throats," answered dirty fingers.

Half a dozen girls squealed.

"Don't be silly," I managed to say before the whole group of 'em broke off into little debates over who these strangers was.

I lost control again. The car'd come to a stop before us an' out climbed the driver. He had that same smirk on his face as when I'd seen him last time. This time he was alone.

"Ain't this nice," he lounged on the hood. "Little Miss Angel playin' the school teacher."

He looked over the kids, who was staring up at him in awe.

His eyes stopped when he got to dirty fingers, who had a defiant look on his face. For a second they stared at each other. Suddenly the driver lunged forward an' poked out his tongue. He laughed to himself as if it was the biggest joke in the world to frighten little kids half out a' their wits.

"Excuse us," I said, tryin' to sound strong. "We're in the middle of a lesson."

He sat on the hood a' the car an' fixed his eyes on me.

"So, lover boy finally got the beatin' he been asking for," he said slyly, completely ignorin' what I jus' said.

"I don't know what you mean," I answered.

I looked across at the kids. Some of the girls was fidgetin' with bits a' twig they'd picked up off a' the ground. The boys was all staring up at this strange dark man who'd come along an' put a stop to our lesson.

"Maybe that's what they mean by divine justice," he chuckled. "Ronny boy gettin' his face smashed in like that."

My eyes was back on him. What was he talkin' 'bout? Ronny was thousands a' miles away, safe on a Greyhound bus.

"Ronny's fine," I said, half to myself. I knew this guy was jus' trying to make me worry. I wasn't gonna get sucked in. "Now will you let us get back to our lesson?" I was beginnin' to feel bad 'bout havin' this part a' my personal life interferin' with my teaching job like this.

"Well, girl," he taunted me, "long as you call thirty stitches in the head an' three broke ribs fine, then I suppose you're right!" With that, he got back into his car an' drove off, roarin' his engine as he disappeared outta the school grounds.

I looked back at the kids, surprised to discover that my eyes'd watered over. They started bombardin' me with questions.

"Who was that ugly creep?"

"Who's Ronny boy?"

"What are stitches?"

I didn't even try to answer. Instead I did my best to get them focused back on our map a' the world. When that failed I told them the lesson was over. Next Sataday we'll be inside no matter how hot it gets, an' please try to pay a little more attention next time.

After the last one'd wandered out a' the gate, I slowly made my way back to the schoolroom, Mister Newton's map a' the world under my arm. Once inside, I folded it up an' put it in his desk drawer. Then I sat down in Mister Newton's chair, leanin' my arms on his desk. I looked 'round the room, a room I thought I knew so well but one I never seen from this angle. I looked at my desk, an' then at the one behind—the one where Ronny used to sit. Sittin' in his chair, I thought of how Mister Newton must've been feelin' in those early days when Ronny'd played up so much. Same way I been feelin' a half hour ago I figured. I wished I was able to handle problem kids as good as he did. I asked myself if I could ever be a real teacher, but before I could answer my mind'd already gone off track. What that driver said 'bout Ronny flashed up in my head. An' then I thought a' the strange way Miss Hattie'd been actin' lately. She'd pretty much told me she was holding somethin' back 'cause she didn't want to hurt me.

Could it be this?

Could it?

I felt a chill run through me. I leaned down on Mister Newton's desk, my head restin' on my arms, an' wondered.

†††

As soon as I got home I went looking for Jimmy. I found him in the kitchen fixin' a peanut butter san'wich. I closed the door so Daddy wouldn't hear us from the living room.

"Jimmy, what do ya know 'bout the freedom rides?" I asked as I sat at the table.

He looked over his shoulder at me. "Come on Angel," he sighed. "You've asked me this before. I've told you what I know. They're travelin' between the states to test out the segregation laws. What else do you want me to say?"

"Have they been attacked?"

"Why ask me?"

"Don't play games with me, Jimmy," I blurted out, a little too loud for comfort.

He turned 'round an', takin' a bite from his san'wich, sat across from me. "Settle down girl," he said. "Now what you goin' on 'bout this for anyway?"

"I think somethin's happened to Ronny," I said quietly.

"Now, is that your head thinkin' or is it your heart worrying?" he asked. I got the feelin' he was makin' fun a' me. I wasn't in the mood for this.

"Jimmy, do you know anythin' or not?"

"Okay." He leaned towards me. "I know somethin' happened when they pulled into Tennessee. But I don't think it was that serious."

"What do ya mean?" I stammered. "What happened?"

"Just some White folks who pushed them 'round a bit. Nothing like what happened to you, though."

He took another bite outta his sandwich. "Don't even worry 'bout it," he added.

"You sure that's all it was?"

"Angel," he lifted his eyes to the ceiling, "this is gettin' boring. Now I told you there's nothing to worry 'bout. Can we leave it at that?"

"Yes Jimmy," I said, still not convinced.

†††

It wasn't until Monday morning that the truth finally came out. An' it was Mister Newton who told it to me. Mister Newton. Sure he wasn't no stranger but he definitely wasn't as close to me as my brother or Miss Hattie were—or least as close as I thought they were. Didn't they think I'd find this out sooner or later? That, when I did, I wish I would a' known it from the start? Or did they still think I was too immature, too babyish, to handle somethin' like this? Mister Newton didn't think I was too babyish. He'd pulled me aside before class an' asked me if I heard what'd happened, heard 'bout the troubles on the bus.

"Not properly," I said, nervously.

"They was attacked in Tennessee on Friday morning," he said softly. "Ronny was involved, but he's fine now, resting in a hospital."

"How bad is he hurt?" I could feel that familiar panic comin' over me again.

"Well, Angel," he said, puttin' his hand on my shoulder, "It was pretty bad. Once he went down they kept at him with their boots."

He moved his hand to my chin now an', guidin' it up so my eyes met his, he said, "But Ronny's one strong boy. He'll be okay. Now are you okay, Angel?"

"Yes Mister Newton," I lied. I paused, then asked, "How many stitches did he need?"

"About thirty," he whispered. "Angel do you want to sit outside for a while?"

I heaved in a breath of air.

"No," I said. "I'll be fine."

I turned an' headed for my desk, careful not to make eye contact with any other kids. But for some reason, I moved past my chair an' slumped myself down at Ronny's desk. I ran my fingers across the edge, as if doin' that would bring me closer to him. Then my eye caught some words that'd been scratched onto the wooden desktop. I read them silently:

I'm sittin behind an angel

"Oh Ronny," I sighed, then quickly looked 'round, hoping nobody'd heard me. All a' kids was busy with their own stuff, no one even noticin' me. Then I looked at the front a' the room, to where Mister Newton was sitting behind his desk. His eyes was beamin' down on me. I knew he could see the tear that'd started rolling down my face but I didn't mind. His smile made it okay

✝✝✝

I sorta moped 'round after school that day. I felt a bit lost, like I didn't quite know where I wanted to be. A'course my heart was tellin' me I had to get to Tennessee to be with Ronny. Then my head was saying to go over to Miss Hattie's place an' fin' out why she'd kept the truth 'bout this from me. But I didn't do neither a' those things. I jus' hung 'round outside a' the class 'til everyone els'd gone, then made my way over to the playin' field an' sat on the rope swing. I pushed myself off so I was able to get a good sway goin' an' then let gravity swing me back an' forwards. I closed my eyes an' tried to pretend I was free, like those two birds I watched out a' my window that other time. I imagined myself drifting along, no longer on the swing, but through the air now. I would glide high up, get myself in line with an air current an' then get swept away. I'd glide right out a' this place, far away from the city a' Birmin'ham, out a' the state a' Alabama. I would drift along on that air current all the way to…

Tennessee.

It seemed like my little imagination games always found a

way to trip me up, to bring me back to whatever it was I was tryin'
to escape from—like the thought a' Ronny lyin' in a hospital bed
in Tennessee with thirty-odd stitches in his face. Oh, how I was
achin' to see him. I needed to look at him, to see for myself that
he was all right. Sure, people could tell me he was all right, but
I knew now that I couldn't trust what they said. They was tryin'
to protect me, but what they was really doin' was makin' me
even more scared. If only I could see Ronny for myself. Then I'd
know how bad he was hurt an' start dealing with that. So, I told
myself, I had to find a way to get to where he was. That was the
only way to go forward.

"You okay, Angel?"

It was Mister Newton. He was lockin' up the schoolroom.
With his bunch a' papers under his arm an' his tie loosened
'round his neck, he looked relieved that his day was over.

"Yes, Mister Newton," I said, lost in thought.

"You thinking about Ronny?" He came towards me.

"Yeah, sorta," I mumbled.

He was right by me now, leanin' on the swing framin'.

"I know it's easy to say this, Angel, but try not to worry
about him. Worrying won't make him any better."

I looked up into his eyes.

"I've got to see him," I said desperately.

He smiled at me. It wasn't that mocking smile like I got from
Jimmy the other day. This smile was one of understandin', like
he knew what I was goin' through.

"Angel," he said, "It's not possible. You're thousands of miles
away from him. An' you've got responsibilities right here."

"Responsibilities like what?"

"Well, like your Saturday class for one."

I groaned.

"I know it seems like the best thing'd be to go to him, Angel, but, even if you did, it could only be for a short time. Then you'd have to part again. Isn't it better to just wait until he comes back for good?"

I didn't answer.

He knelt down beside me.

"Anyway," he said, "You can always write to him. That way your words will be with him all the time. He can read them over an' over. How about that?"

"I guess so."

I must've sounded unconvinced. But then I remembered the letter I begun the other day, the letter that was still sittin' in my schoolbag.

"Mister Newton, how can I get a letter to Ronny in that hospital?" I asked.

"Well," he said, "Miss Hattie Milton has been in communication with him. Think you can get an address off her?"

I knew it. That old girl was mixed up in the middle a' this all along. I had to face up to her, to find out why she'd been actin' so secret with me.

"Oh, yes," I said. "I'm sure I can."

†††

I foun' her sittin' on her balcony, peelin' 'taters.

"I was hopin' somebody'd come along an' share this job with me," she said as I joined her in the shade.

"Ain't here to do that," I replied. I didn't want to waste any time in lettin' her know what was on my mind. She stopped peelin' an' looked at me.

"Oh, really?" she said, raisin' an eyebrow.

"Miss Hattie, why didn't ya tell me 'bout Ronny?"

She began peelin' another tater.

"Because I promised I wouldn't," she said softly.

"Promised who?" I demanded.

She looked across at me.

"Ronny," she said.

I was confused.

"You mean you spoke to him?"

"Not quite."

She let the peels drop into her lap.

"I had a phone call from Jim Bevel, Friday lunchtime. He told me what'd happened to Ronny. An' he told me that Ronny made him promise to tell me not to tell you what'd happened."

"Why would he do that?" I asked.

"Why do you think, Angel?"

I didn't answer.

She reached for another tater.

"Because he cares 'bout you, girl."

I sat in silence for a few moments, lettin' this sink in.

"You know how bad he was hurt?" I finally asked.

"Not really," she said.

"Well, what else did Jim say?"

"He jus' asked me to let Ronny's mother know what'd happened. So, that's what I did."

"You went to his mother's place?"

"Uh huh."

She stood up now an' collected all the peels together in her apron.

"How'd you find out 'bout Ronny anyhow?" she demanded.

"Mister Newton told me."

She emptied her apron over the trashcan in the corner a' the balcony.

"How you feeling 'bout it?" she asked.

"Like I wanna be beside him."

"He wouldn't even let you see him, Angel." She looked at me. Her next words was slow an' deliberate as if she wanted me to remember them. "He loves you so much that he'd deny himself the comfort a' having you there so you won't get hurt."

"But I need to see him, to know he's…"

"Angel," she cut me off, "Ronny loves you enough to deny himself. Do you love him that much?"

She'd moved back alongside me now. She was bending down to scoop up the bowl a' taters, but her eyes was still fixed on me.

"Yes, Miss Hattie," I whimpered.

"Then you'll wait," she said firmly. With that, she disappeared into the house.

✝✝✝

Deny myself. That's what I did over the next few weeks. It was real hard, but it was what Ronny wanted, so I did it. I didn't talk no more 'bout wanting to go to him. Didn't really talk 'bout him at all. I knew if I was gonna get through this time, I had to try to focus on other things—my school work, my Sataday teachin' job, the latest news on what Doctor King was up to. So, that's what I did. It helped me get through the days, but the nights was another story. I'd lie in bed, hopin' that sleep'd come quickly, but it never would. Instead, I would see an image a' Ronny on the ground, his face covered in blood, his hands protectin' his head an' a boot poundin' into him. The picture was so real I wasn't sure if I was imaginin' what'd happened to Ronny or if I was rememberin' what'd happened to me. Anyway, Ronny'd be takin' this savage beatin' an' then he'd yell out, "Angel!" as if he was wantin' me to come an' save him. But I couldn't.

It was the same nightmare every night. 'Cept I didn't even have to fall asleep to have it. It seemed to know jus' when to come, when to haunt me—the minute my head hit that pillow. So, I took to sittin' up on my bed until I felt drowsy an', I hoped, ready to drift off to sleep. I began readin' more outta the Bible. An' I wrote letters to Ronny. Then one night, when I didn't feel like doin' neither a' those things, I decided to slip back downstairs an' get the newspaper. I found it by Daddy's armchair, all pulled apart an' folded in half. I gathered the different sections together an' headed back to my room. I sat on my bed an' started goin' through it, lookin' for anythin' excitin'. Most a' the news was borin' stuff 'bout the Birmin'ham Ratepayers Committee an' the City Roading Commission. Why do adults get so caught up with committees an' commissions, I wondered, ready to give up on the paper all together. But then somethin' caught my eye. It was the tiniest of articles an' it was on 'bout page eighteen. It read:

MARCH ON WASHINGTON
Negro leader A. Philip Randolph announced today a proposal for a march on Washington, D.C. in support of the passage of a civil rights bill. The date of such was given as Wednesday, August 28. There has been a mixed reaction in the Negro community while among the general populace a fear of repetition of the recent negroid violence has given rise to a feeling of uneasiness about the whole affair.

A march on Washin'ton. That was big. I leaned back against the wall an' thought 'bout what it could be like. I imagined an army a' people, people without guns, without hate, Black an' White together, comin' from all over the country an' marching on up to the gates a' President Kennedy's White House. A'course, Doctor King'd be way up front an' he'd speak for the millions a' people. He'd ask the President for equal rights. Then the President'd look out over the sea a' people an' with a wave a' his hand he'd pass all the laws we needed to be equal. To be free.

An' I would be there to see it happen.

Then I told myself to stop bein' foolish. That ain't the way it works. Lord knows, I learnt that lesson well enough. You can pass all the laws you want, but it can't change what's in folk's hearts. But one thing I knew for sure. Whatever happened at that March on Washin'ton on August 28th, I was gonna be there to see it.

✝✝✝

We was goin' to Washin'ton. This was 'bout the biggest thing my family'd ever done. But when the news 'bout that march came out, an' folks started talkin' 'bout if they was gonna go, my Daddy'd made it plain from the start that his family was gonna be there. What's missin' a day's wages compared to bein' a part a' history he'd said. I guess Daddy'd got himself swept along with the excitement of what'd been goin' on over the last few months. What he'd first seen as a good excuse to get ya head busted had turned into a real victory for Black folks an' now the whole world was paying attention. I think that'd surprised Daddy. But it was a good surprise an' now I felt like he was where he should've been all along—on our side. But if Daddy'd come on over to our side, Mama sure hadn't. She was wary 'bout the whole march on Washin'ton thing from the start. Folks ain't gonna give up good wages an' pay the money to get there, she'd scoffed. An' what happens if only a few hundred people showed up, instead a' the thousands they'd been talking 'bout? They'd all look foolish an' the cameras would beam pictures a' those foolish niggers right 'round the world. Might as well forget the whole thing, she said, an' to me it sounded more like a command than a suggestion.

But I had no intention a' forgettin' it. In fact, as each day passed by, I got more an' more excited 'bout it, imaginin' what it

was gonna be like. An' then, before I knew it, the day'd arrived—
August 28, 1963. Daddy'd got me outta bed at 'bout three in the
morning. I dressed quickly, my best dress laid out from the night
before. I polished my shoes too, shining them until I could see a
reflection offa the toe. I hardly managed to wipe the sleep from
my eyes, before the three of us—Daddy, Jimmy an' me—were
makin' our way to the corner of our street where an old school
bus was waitin'. The bus was already half filled by the time we
got there, an' no sooner had I slumped down on a seat besides
my brother than it started it's engine an' began crawlin' down
the street. We was on our way.

I tried to drift back to sleep, but the constant bumpin' a'
that bus, along with the buzz a' noise from those seated 'round
me, kept me half-awake. I spent the first few hours a' that trip
dreamily staring out the window, watching the darkened shapes
that was Harpersville, Birmin'ham an' Alabama disappear
behind us. As daylight came, I was able to make out the road
signs that simply read SOUTH. A'course they was on the
other side a' the road, an' each one we passed seemed to me
like another link in the chain a' Black oppression that was
bein' pulled apart. We was leavin' that—leavin' the South. I
wondered if it really was a different world up north-if it really
was a world where color didn't matter. I doubted that there'd
be any place like that anywhere in the whole world, let alone
here in America. America, where a thirteen year old girl could
get herself half beaten to death in broad daylight an' then get
arrested for it, all 'cause she jus' happened to be Black.

"Have a look at this," my brother interrupted my thoughts. He
was pushin' a piece a' paper in front a' my face. I looked 'round
the bus to see that most everyone else was lookin' over a copy a'
the same piece a' paper. I took hold a' the page an' began readin':

REMINDERS FOR WASHINGTON MARCHERS

The Washington March is a living petition—in the flesh—of the scores of thousands of citizens of both races who will be present from all parts of the country.

It will be orderly but not subservient. It will be proud but not arrogant. It will be non-violent but not timid. It will be unified in purposes and behavior, not splintered into groups and individual competitors. It will be outspoken but not raucous.

It will have the dignity befitting a demonstration on behalf of the human rights of 20 millions of people, with the eye and judgment of the world focused upon Washington, D.C., on August 28,1963. In a neighborly dispute, there may be stunts, rough words and even hot insults, but when a whole people speaks to its government, the dialogue and the action must be on a level reflecting the worth of that people and the responsibility of that government.

We, therefore, remind all marchers that we must resist provocation to disorder and violence. Evil persons are determined to smear this march. We must have the self-discipline so that no one in our ranks, however enthusiastic, shall be the spark for disorder.

There was more, but the overall message was the same: self-discipline, self-pride, non-violence. Yet, even though this message was a positive one, my eyes was drawn back to one sentence, a sentence that made me uneasy 'bout what was ahead—evil persons are determined to smear this march.

†††

"Angel."

My eyes flickered open. Jimmy was nudgin' me awake. I wasn't sure jus' when I drifted off to sleep. Last thing I remembered was the rolling hills a' the countryside disappearing behind us as we sped along some highway in the middle a' Tennessee. I felt my heart poundin' the second I realized what state we was in. Ronny was here. But it was the strangest feelin'. I almost felt guilty that I didn't want to stop here to be with him. The excitement 'bout the march'd taken over an' now all I wanted to do was to get to that Washin'ton monument an' be a part of whatever it was that lay ahead. So I guess I was glad that sleep finally come to me—sleep meant not feelin' guilty 'bout Ronny an' it meant we'd be there sooner.

I rubbed my eyes an' looked 'round.

"Why we goin' so slow, Jimmy?" I asked.

"Look out the window," my brother replied.

I did as he said. Alongside us was another bus. I could see it was full a' Black folks, jus' like ours. I strained my neck to look beyond that bus, only to see another in front of it. The same thing behind.

"A traffic jam," I whispered.

"We're in a line a' fifty seven buses, Angel," Jimmy said. "The drivers've been radioing each other, keepin' a tally. Not bad huh?"

I squeezed my brother's arm.

"Jimmy," I said, "It's really happenin'."

Jimmy nodded slowly.

"Now we gotta pray that all of these people can stand together as one," he said.

The bus convoy crawled on for another half hour. Finally, we wormed our way onto a paddock an' parked up, one in a line a' 'bout thirty Greyhound buses. As Jimmy an' I waited for the others to climb off a' the bus, I looked over the number plates of the buses an' cars that was sprawled across the paddock. In five minutes, I read more state names than I knew existed. Then it was time for us to get outta the bus. As I stepped out an' down onto the ground, I made a mental note that this was my first taste a' northern air. An' it tasted good. Not like the stiflin' heat a' the air back home. That air could half choke you but this, this air was clean. It was fresh. It was free.

We joined an ever growin' crowd who was makin' their way outta the parking area an' along a narrow street. I clung onto Daddy's hand as we merged into a sea a' people. The crowd that stretched out before us was spillin' outta the main street down into the side alleys. It was more people than I ever even imagined bein' together in one place. Those behind us was inching us slowly forward. Bein' in the middle a' so many people, I kinda felt powerless, as if all I could do was to flow along with them. But then I felt the tightness of a grip on my arm. I looked across at my brother.

"Come on," he whispered, pulling me back against the flow a' the crowd.

"What are ya doin'?" I yelled.

"Come with me," he demanded.

I looked up at Daddy, on the other side a' me. He nodded his head.

"Go," he said.

So, Jimmy fought his way back, duckin', swervin' an' jostlin' past untold bodies until he'd finally got us into a side alley. The crowd'd thinned out some back there. At least I had room to lean against a brick building.

"What you do that for?" I demanded.

"You'll see." An' with that, he was draggin' me down the alley. We disappeared 'round another corner. Across the street from us was a park. People was walking across it, eager to join the crowd we'd jus' escaped from.

"Look over there," Jimmy was pointing at three guys gathered 'round a park bench. I noticed one of 'em was in a wheelchair. That one had his back to me, but one a' the others was starin' right at us.

"Isn't that Jim Bevel?" I asked.

"Go over," Jimmy pushed me forward.

"What?"

"Go," he ordered.

Nervously, I made my way across the street. I felt kind a' foolish. I had no idea why I was approaching these guys or what I was gonna say. Half way across I turned to look back at Jimmy. He'd disappeared. Oh great, I thought, jus' great. But then I began closin' in on the three of 'em. Jim Bevel was smilin' at me. I studied the back a' the head in that wheelchair an' all of a sudden somethin' clicked.

"Ronny," I whispered.

I could feel my hands sweatin' as I got closer. I was only a few feet away from that wheelchair now. I was 'bout to call out to him when the wheelchair began to slowly turn.

"You trying to sneak up on me, Angel?"

I hadn't heard that voice for two months, but at that moment it was like we'd never been apart. I rushed forward an' threw myself down beside him. Tears welled up in my eyes as he guided my head onto his lap an' caressed my face.

"Oh, Ronny," I whimpered.

"It's all right," he said softly.

"I love you so much," I blubbered, grabbing onto his hand. I didn't care that I must've been makin' a fool a' myself before the others. I had Ronny back. Nothin' else mattered. His hand moved to my chin, an' he guided it up so that I was lookin' into his face.

"Even like this?" he whispered.

Ronny's face was a mess. The cheekbone on one side was a couple inches too high. His chin had a cleft in it that wasn't there before an' his nose was crooked. An' then there was his eye. The right one. It was completely closed over. I had to force myself not to wince. But Ronny's face could've been blown right off for all the difference it made to me.

"Yes," I smiled through the tears. "Oh, yes, Ronny."

He tightened his grip on my hand.

"Angel," he whispered, "I wasn't no coward this time."

I reached up an' ran my hand along his cheek. I felt the wetness of a tear.

"You never were," I comforted him. "Not to me."

He quickly looked 'round to see how close those two other guys were. When he was sure they was a safe distance away, he turned back to me.

"But I was to me," he mumbled. He looked down at the ground, the same way he used to when he didn't feel good enough to look me in the eye.

"Angel," he said, "I felt ashamed to stand next to you. I wasn't worthy of it."

I sighed, trying to think what I could say to him. Is this really why he went away, why he put himself on the front lines? Did he want to get beat up jus' so he could prove to himself that he was as good as me? I knew that was wrong, but I knew it also proved jus' how much he needed me. An' that made it all right. I grabbed his chin an' guided his eyes back towards mine, the same way he'd done to me jus' a minute before.

"You crazy fool," I said.

An' then I kissed him.

†††

The sun beat down without letup on that massive crowd. It reflected offa the waters a' the Memorial Pool alongside us. I had to squint as I peered up at the man, way in the distance, who was standin' behind the microphones. The crowd kinda parted for us when I pushed Ronny back over here. It seemed like they'd looked at Ronny 'n jus' knew how he'd got so messed up. So they'd moved aside outta respect. Anyway, we'd managed to get right alongside the Memorial Pool. An' here we were. I was hangin' onto Ronny's hand, not daring to let go. Didn't dare risk letting him outta reach again.

I couldn't really make out much a' the man behind the podium. Could see he was young an' had dark hair. But I could sure hear him. Could hear the anger in his words, the impatience in his tone. I can remember him saying we was gonna keep right on marchin', keep goin', keep resistin' until we got some real progress. I can't remember what else he said but I got the clear impression that this guy was frustrated. I bent down to Ronny.

"Do you know him?"

"That's John Lewis," he replied. "Leader a' SNICK. Came to see me in the hospital."

Then, noticin' I didn't seem too impressed with this John Lewis, he added, "He's cool, Angel."

Soon John Lewis was replaced on the podium by a shorter, older man. He was there to introduce the man we'd all been waitin' to hear, the man he called the moral leader of our nation. As he made way for that speaker a hush swept across the mass a' people. That other man stepped up to the podium. For a minute he stood in silence, as if taken back by the size a' the crowd sprawled out before him. When he finally did speak, his voice was even more powerful than the last time I heard it. It was what I imagined rich, dark chocolate would sound like:

"I am happy to join with you today in what will go down in history as the greatest demonstration for freedom in the history of our nation.

"Five score years ago, a great American, in whose symbolic shadow we stand, signed the Emancipation Proclamation. This momentous decree came as a great beacon of hope to millions of Negro slaves, who had been seared in the flames of withering injustice. It came as a joyous daybreak to end the long night of their captivity. But one hundred years later the Negro still is not free. One hundred years later, the life of the Negro is still sadly crippled by the manacle of segregation and the chains of discrimination..."

Martin's words took me away. An' as I clung to Ronny's hand I looked into the future with him...

"Nineteen sixty three is not an end but a beginning. Those who hope that the Negro needed to blow off steam and will now be content will have a rude awakening if the nation returns to business as usual. ..."

"No, no we are not satisfied until justice rolls down like waters and righteousness like a mighty stream. ...

"Let us not wallow in the valley of despair. I say to you today, my friends, that even though we face the difficulties of today and tomorrow, I still have a dream. It is a dream deeply rooted in the American dream."

"I have a dream that one day this nation will rise up and live out the true meaning of its creed—we hold these truths to be self-evident that all men are born equal. I have a dream that one day on the red hills of Georgia the sons of former slaves and the sons of former slave owners will be able to sit down together at the table of brotherhood. I have a dream that one day even the state of Mississippi, a state sweltering with the heat of injustice, sweltering with the heat of oppression, will be transformed into an oasis of freedom and justice. I have a dream that my four little children will one day live in a nation where they will not be judged by the color of their skin but by the content of their character."

"I have a dream today!"

"I have a dream that one day, down in Alabama, with its vicious racists, with its governor having his lips dripping with the words of interposition and nullification: one day right down in Alabama little Black boys and Black girls will be able to join hands with little White boys and White girls as sisters and brothers."

"I have a dream today!"

"I have a dream that one day every valley shall be exalted, and every hill and mountain shall be made low, the rough places will be made plain and the crooked places will be made straight and the glory of the Lord shall be revealed and all flesh shall see it together. ... And when this happens, when we allow freedom to ring, when we let it ring from every tenement and every hamlet, from every state and every city, we will be able to speed up that day when all of God's children, Black men and White men, Jews and Gentiles, Protestants and Catholics, will be able to join hands and sing in the words of the old Negro spiritual, 'Free at last, free at last. Thank God Almighty we are free at last.'"

When Martin finished speakin' he stepped back an' waited. I was so taken away by his words that I was caught off guard by the thunderous applause that erupted all 'round me. Hundreds a' thousands a' pairs a' hands let him know that they shared his dream too. In my mind at that moment, Martin Lutha' King was the greatest man on earth. An' standing there, letting the power a' his words sink into my brain, anythin' seemed possible. It took me back to how I felt that day in school when I seen my picture in the Los Angeles Times. Back then I felt like I could do anythin'. But now, as I looked 'round, I saw that the power didn't come from jus' me—it came from hundreds a' thousands jus' like me. The energy from all a' those people that day lifted me like never before, an' for the first time in a long while I felt good 'bout the future.

Chapter NINE
ALABAMA, SEPTEMBER 15 1963

"Is Ronny comin', Miss Angel?" Denise asked as I helped slip her choir gown over her head.

It was 10:15 on Sunday mornin' at the Sixteenth Street Church. I promised a couple a' the girls in my Sataday class that I'd come along to watch 'em sing in the Youth Day choir. It was a special day for the girls an' they was real excited 'bout it. An' they all wanted Ronny to be there to share it with 'em.

Ronny'd taken to comin' along on Satadays with me to class. He was so good with those kids that sometimes I felt jus' a little jealous that I couldn't build up that same sorta relationship with 'em. He'd laugh an' joke with the boys an' tease the girls. But he still always had 'em under control. It was the way Mister Newton was with us—free an' easy but we always knew who was boss. On those Sataday afternoons I saw a new side a' Ronny. I saw he had the makings of a great teacher. So I was never surprised when the first question they'd ask me was, "Where's Ronny?"

"Sure he'll be here," I smiled, zippin' up her gown. "Said he wouldn't miss it."

Denise turned to face me.

"Tell me what it was like, Miss Angel, when you was on that march."

I sat down on the bench alongside her.

"Well," I began thinkin' out loud. "I was real nervous at the start. But you know, when I saw all those angry White people it made me so mad that my nervousness jus' went away."

"I could never be so strong as you," she looked up at me admiringly.

"Sure you could. All it takes is a good heart. An' I know you got that."

"Ronny's comin', Miss Angel," Addie Mae called from the other side a' the room.

I looked up through the basement window to see Ronny wheeling himself up to the church steps.

"Better help him," I said cheerily. I smiled at the group a' girls in the basement. "Back in a minute."

I skipped up the steps an' out the church doors.

"Need a hand?" I called out as I ran to Ronny.

He never got to answer. A massive blast ripped away our peacefulness. It picked me up an' smashed me onto the sidewalk. I felt a pain in my arm as it was pinned under my body. Then a rain a' dust an' shattered brick fell over me. I looked across at Ronny. His wheelchair had been thrown backwards, an' he was sprawled on the road a half dozen feet away from it. He was calling to me.

"Angel, are you all right?"

"Don't know," I stumbled to my feet.

I tasted blood from the side a' my face. My eyes was stung with smoke that was pouring outta the church doors. I tried to make it over to Ronny.

"Get away from the building," Ronny screamed as people began emergin' through the smoke. I watched as a woman with a baby in her arms was pulled out the door. She struggled free an' ran back in. Finally, she was dragged out onto the street.

"My baby's in there," she screamed.

Then I recognized her. It was Denise's mother. Oh no, I thought. The girls in the basement. I looked down towards the bottom a' the church, where I been standin' only a few minutes ago. It had completely caved in. There could be no escape from that.

In a daze, I stumbled to where Ronny lay. I tried to help him up but fell over myself. Two men saw us lyin' on the ground an' came over to help. They soon had Ronny sittin' back in his wheelchair. They moved us along with the rest a' the folks who was lucky enough to get outta that church. Soon, we was down at Kelley Ingram Park, a safe distance away. I could hear the emergency sirens bearing down on the church. Too late, I thought. Always, too late. Some a' the people was hysterical. A man was yellin' out, to nobody in particular, "Not in the Lords house—hell, not in the Lords house."

Women was cryin' uncontrollably. Ronny an' I jus' sat there starin'. It seemed unreal. Too terrible to be real. But I felt the blood still runnin' down my cheek an' knew it was. The news began to filter through that the four girls in the basement — Denise, Cynthia, Addie Mae an' Carole —were dead. Within moments I saw the shock a' those people turn to anger. Men began attackin' whatever they could find—a trashcan, street signs, a car. I looked across at Ronny.

"What are we gonna do, Ronny?"

He looked back at me, as if he hadn't even been aware a' me bein' there. He reached his hand across an' wiped the blood from my face.

"Angel, he said, "this is the darkest hour. We've come through the night. All we gotta do is keep our head. The dawn's jus' 'round the corner."

"Do you really believe that?" I said, lookin' out at the madness before us.

"I've got to," he whispered, "an' so do you. If we don't, then everythin' we've done is for nothin'. But, Angel, it ain't for nothin'. Josiah Reeby wasn't for nothin'. Your broke arm wasn't for nothin'. An' this here wheelchair ain't for nothin', either."

He reached for my hand.

"This was because the White folks are desperate, Angel. They know we've won. Best they can do is blow up one of our churches on a Sunday morning. Girl, we've got 'em beat."

I smiled at him then. Four little girls, girls with big dreams an' high expectations, had jus' been killed, my community was goin' crazy an', still, Ronny Jackson had made me smile.

"How'd you get to be so smart?" I asked.

He looked me full in the eyes. For a moment he didn't speak, jus' stared at me, not even blinkin'.

"Had me a good teacher," he finally replied.